Writing Clementine

Writing Clementine

Kate Gordon

ALLEN&UNWIN
SYDNEY • MELBOURNE • AUCKLAND • LONDON

This project has been assisted by the Australian Government through the Australia Council for the Arts, its arts funding and advisory body.

Australian Government

Australia Council for the Arts

This project was assisted through Arts Tasmania by the Minister for the Arts.

First published in 2014

Allen & Unwin
83 Alexander Street
Crows Nest NSW 2065
Australia
Phone: (61 2) 8425 0100
Email: info@allenandunwin.com
Web: www.allenandunwin.com

A Cataloguing-in-Publication entry is available from
the National Library of Australia
www.trove.nla.gov.au

ISBN 978 1 74331 663 4

'The Good Morrow' by John Donne on page 4 first published in his collection *Songs and Sonnets*, 1633
HG Wells quote on page 156 is from *The Fate of Man: An Unemotional Statement of the Things That Are Happening to Him Now, and of the Immediate Possibilities Confronting Him*, 1939

Cover and text design by Kirby Armstrong
Cover images: teapot © Nuiiko / Shutterstock; title notepaper © Picsfive / Shutterstock; background spots © daisybee / Shutterstock; heart © Valentyn Volkov / Shutterstock; girl © BestPhotoStudio / Shutterstock; frame © PinkPueblo / Shutterstock; hat © vandervelden / iStockphoto
Set in 11/14 pt Adobe Garamond Pro by Midland Typesetters, Australia
Printed in Australia by McPherson's Printing Group

10 9 8 7 6 5 4 3 2 1

FSC www.fsc.org MIX Paper from responsible sources FSC® C001695

The paper in this book is FSC certified.
FSC promotes en vironmentally responsible, socially beneficial and economically viable management of the world's forests.

For Mr Hiller, for making me believe in things I never thought possible, and for Tiger, for making me believe in magic

Dear Ms Hiller,

Last night I had the strangest dream.

It was my first day of Grade 9. I came to class, and instead of chairs and tables in the classroom, there was an enormous swimming pool. Instead of a teacher behind a desk, there was a strange sea creature – like an oversized anemone, I suppose, or a huge sea sponge. And all the other kids in my class were already in the pool, floating calmly.

Now I was in the pool, too. But I was not floating, Ms Hiller. I was struggling. I splashed frantically towards the anemone and I asked it, *Where should I go? What should I do? How do I stay afloat?* The anemone didn't answer, and I was terrified, because I wasn't sure at all how to be, and I was worried that if I didn't work it out, I'd drown.

I'm not sure why I am writing this, except that when we came in, you said only one word: 'Write.'

It's my first day of Grade 9, Ms Hiller, and I'm not in a pool and you're not an anemone . . . but I still don't know what to do.

The whole class seemed bewildered. It wasn't only me. But I was the only one who raised her hand to ask what exactly you *wanted* us to write.

'What's your name?' you asked me.

'Clementine,' I answered.

You nodded and smiled and said, 'Write about her. Write Clementine.'

And after that I couldn't think of anything to say, so I sat with my mouth opening and closing, like a goldfish.

My sister, Sophie, was in your philosophy class when *she* was in Grade 9. She'd come home after your lessons and tell me all about Foucault and Alain de Botton. I read de Botton's book *Essays in Love* after Sophie told me I should. It was all about love's endings and beginnings, and it fascinated me. It made me think about what it might be like, to fall properly in love.

Sophie loaned me Foucault, as well. He's less accessible, but I'm sure I *could* understand him. If somebody taught me how.

You are meant to *teach* me, aren't you, Ms Hiller? You're not meant to come into class on the first day and say, 'Write.'

Blue fish, red fish, green fish . . .

That's what you said to write, if our heads were empty, until they filled again.

Blue fish, red fish, green fish . . .

It's not only *my* mind that is deserted. In case you can't see, Ms Hiller, Gemma Gleave is texting under her desk. Clarissa Docklands is drawing butterflies on her arm. Gryff Willcox and Waylon Ogilvie are passing notes to each other and sniggering.

A few of the others are writing, but I can see that Shelley Peterson is doing her maths homework, and Ioannis Poulos is probably working on song lyrics for his band, Joseph's Trench Coat.

Blue fish, red fish, green fish . . .

None of us is learning philosophy. You can't learn anything by writing about fish.

You said you'll only read our writing if we want you to; that you'll understand if we wish to keep it private.

If we want to, we can pass it in, once a week. Aren't you curious, though, Ms Hiller, to find out what we're writing about?

I am.

I want to know if anyone is writing anything good. Proper writing. That's what I want to do, Ms Hiller. Proper writing. Poetry.

I know it isn't exactly *fashionable*, and you can't make a career out of being a poet, or so my sister says. But I enjoy it. I love balancing words on top of words as if they're bricks and I'm a builder, laying the mortar between them so they form something beautiful; making the foggy thoughts that swish and swirl around inside me into something solid.

Making sense of life.

My poems are in a box beneath my bed. When the box fills, I empty it into a suitcase in my wardrobe. A suitcase full of folded thoughts.

And every time I think I might pull them out and look at them again, or show them to someone else, I open a book and I read.

Sylvia Plath. John Donne. Les Murray.

They're my favourites, Ms Hiller. They were the poets who first prodded at my heart. John Donne's 'The Good-morrow' is my most loved poem of all time.

I wonder by my troth, what thou and I
Did, till we loved. Were we not wean'd till then?
But suck'd on country pleasures, childishly?
Or snorted we in the Seven Sleepers' den? 'Twas so; but
this, all pleasures fancies be;
If ever any beauty I did see,
Which I desired, and got, 'twas but a dream of thee.

It's about never having really lived until you meet the one you love. As if the whole rest of your life is a dream, up to the moment someone – *the* one – wakes you from it.

That's what I imagine it to be like.

Love.

And that's what I want to do with my poetry: capture exactly how things *are*. Use words to make *concrete* my imaginings. Catch love. Catch happiness. Tie things down.

I'll never be able to do it as well as John Donne, but when I'm a hundredth as good, maybe then I'll open the suitcase.

Blue fish, red fish, green fish . . .

It's our second day here, Ms Hiller, and when we came in, you said, 'Write.'

In English we've already started reading our set texts. In my art history elective, Mrs Jermy is teaching us about Louise Bourgeois. In studies of society and environment we've made a list of topical issues in the news and have each been assigned one to research.

I have spent the past thirty-four minutes staring at my notebook. It's like an empty city. The lines are deserted alleyways, and I feel alone here.

Ms Hiller, there are six minutes left of class. Can you tell me something? Anything? Something about life or love?

Ms Hiller?

Why am I here?

Today I want to write about a strange thing that happened.

Don't get too excited, Ms Hiller. It isn't flying-saucer strange or Loch Ness monster strange. But it's strange enough to be tickling my mind still, almost a whole day later.

It happened on the sports oval, after school yesterday.

I was on a Run of Doom.

Runs of Doom happen every couple of days, and they happen because my friends think I'm fat. They haven't told me that, explicitly, but I know the truth. They are trying to 'help' me lose weight by taking me running around the oval. They pretend the running is for them, but it isn't. They're trying to 'fix' me. They jog next to me, shouting encouragement; telling me that I am doing good. I think they've been watching too many television weight-loss shows.

I hate the Runs of Doom.

Firstly, the actual running is *boring*. Secondly, I hate the reason behind it. I hate that my friends want to change me.

Chelsea-Grace and Cleo think the body size of most Hollywood movie stars represents the average woman. They think Taylor Swift has a figure to aspire to. They don't understand that some of us are never going to look like that and that's *fine* and actually *good*, because wouldn't the world be *boring* if we did all look like Taylor Swift? I don't *mind* being a size fourteen. I don't want to be super-thin like they are.

I don't want to wear tight skirts and boob tubes. I like my jeans and jumpers. I look at the skinny girls in the magazines and, while some of them are beautiful, I know I'd look funny if I was that slender. I'm not meant to look like that.

Also, I like eating; I don't want to starve myself. The people I look up to aren't the glamorous celebrities in the magazines. The life I'm aiming for isn't dependent on a certain size of trousers. Writers are admired for their brains and their words. Nobody cares if they have wobbly bits or crazy hair or wonky noses.

Which is exactly as it should be.

But Cleo and Chelsea-Grace don't think so. And so they make me run. And as I run, around and around, I become more and more grumpy, and they seem to me more and more like horrible motivational speakers from some trashy television show, until after a while I don't recognise them anymore, and a while after that, I don't recognise myself.

And so it goes. Every few days. Always the same.

Except for yesterday. Yesterday, something changed.

Yesterday, there was a boy.

He was sitting on the hill behind the sports field, under the big cider-gum tree, and he was drinking tea, poured from a china pot into a tiny china cup.

And he was dressed like Sherlock Holmes.

I watched the new, strange boy for so long that Chelsea-Grace ran backwards, grabbed my hand and pulled me towards her. 'What are you staring at, hon?' she asked. 'Not that crazy guy up there? Who is he? Is he new? He looks like a total freakazoid! Oh, oops. I mean . . .'

Chelsea-Grace has this new thing. She read in a magazine somewhere that good people look prettier; that their 'inner virtue' gives them a glow that mean people don't have. So Chelsea-Grace is trying to be good. Which is difficult for her because, while she's never mean on purpose, Chels does have a bit of a problem with talking before she thinks. The effort of trying to be Snow White makes her face flush and her cheeks puff out, as if all the little catty 'truths' she's holding in have turned to marbles in her mouth.

The ironic thing is that with her long, wavy dark hair and peaches-and-cream skin, Chelsea-Grace could easily play Snow White in a pantomime, if only she traded her skin-tight floral mini-dresses and jelly sandals for a flouncy princess dress and velvet-bow shoes. (Unlikely to happen.) Looks-wise, she doesn't need to change one bit: she's beautiful. She's the only one who doesn't know it.

'Of course she's not staring at him,' Cleo answered for me, adjusting the sparkly clip holding the fringe of her edgy blonde bob away from her face. If Chelsea-Grace is Snow White, Cleo is Sleeping Beauty, albeit with a much more modern haircut and skin by St Tropez. 'As if anyone would stare at *him*. He's bizarre. He . . . Does he have a picnic basket?'

She was right, Ms Hiller. The boy *did* have a picnic basket. A cane one, with a red cover. And he had a red picnic rug as well.

'Plus, he's not good-looking enough to perv on, is he?' said Chelsea-Grace. 'Sorry if that sounds rude, but it's the truth. So it's not rude. Is it? Is it rude if it's the truth?' Chelsea-Grace seemed to have arrived at a genuinely complex moral crossroads. I decided to leave her there.

'He doesn't look so bad.' I sneaked another glance, taking in his deerstalker hat and the strange tweed cape he wore. It looked vintage. As if it might be his grandfather's. It was definitely odd. But it was *intriguing*.

As I was watching, the boy looked up. Even from a distance I could see that his eyes were *piercing*.

And then the strange thing happened.

He smiled at me.

And it was a nice smile.

I would have smiled back, only Cleo took my hand this time, and yanked me along, with a roll of her eyes and an irritated grunt, and before I knew it I was running again. 'Don't worry, Clem. You may never find a guy as hot as my Todd—'

'Who isn't even your Todd,' Chelsea-Grace interrupted, poking her tongue out.

'*Yet*,' Cleo said, with emphasis. 'But he will be. And we'll find Clem someone who is nearly as hot, or at least better than that weirdo. Don't lower your standards, Clemmie. Keep running.'

And so I did. Inside my head I mimed sword fights and pistol duels with the girls who were meant to be my best ever friends. But on the outside, I kept running. By the time we came back around the boy was gone. And I grew more and more grumpy, and Cleo and Chelsea-Grace became more and more like horrible motivational speakers, until after a while I didn't recognise them anymore, and a while after that, I didn't recognise myself.

My First Memory
by Clementine Darcy

We have a topic to write about today! I admit I'm glad you'll be giving us a theme from time to time. Most days not much happens in the life of Clementine Darcy, so 'Writing Clementine' could become quite dull for all involved. Memories are easier to write about. They're already there – stories behind a closed door in your mind, waiting to be told.

My first memory is only a fragment. A smell, a few words and a *feeling*.

When I was three years old, Mum and Dad and Fergus and Sophie went to Hong Kong. I had to stay behind, with my Aunty Debbie. It wasn't their fault. There was a problem with my vaccinations, and they didn't discover it until it was too late to cancel everything. Don't be alarmed, Ms Hiller. Mum says I was thrilled to be staying with my aunty and my cousins. I packed a little pink suitcase and everything.

It was an adventure. This isn't a sad story, Ms Hiller.

My first memory is not of them leaving. I don't remember that at all. What I remember is them coming back.

I was in Aunty Debbie's sunroom, at the front of her house, and the light was pink because it was sunset. I was sitting on the floor. The door flew open, and Fergus ran in. He picked me up and he held me to him, so tightly. He smelled of peanut butter. He whispered in my ear, 'I missed you, little sister, and I won't ever leave you again.'

And I felt safe.

That's all. That's all I remember. Now, it's all I can do not to go up to his room and slap him and yell. Because he lied.

Nothing about Alain de Botton, Ms Hiller?

Nothing about life? Nothing about love?

Only: 'Write.'

Is this the way it will always be? Will we never learn anything?

Today, the whiteboard was completely clean.

'I have nothing to write about, Ms Hiller,' Gryff whined.

You looked up, for a moment. 'Write about what you did last night.'

'I'm not sure you'd want to read it,' Gryff said, smiling smugly.

'You're probably right,' you said. You opened your book again. Gryff turned red.

You wouldn't want to read about my night either, Ms Hiller. Because what I did last night was nothing at all. Nothing important or philosophical. It was an ordinary night.

Well. There *were* Tim Tams, I suppose. That's something.

We bought them on the way home from school. Dad gave me a lift, and we stopped at the shops and bought chicken mince and tomatoes. Dad stifled a naughty-boy grin as he sneaked in a packet of Double Choc Vanillas.

'Don't tell your mother,' he said.

In the car, for the rest of the way, we listened to Jimmy Buffett. You mightn't have heard of him, because it's 'Dad' music, and I wouldn't recommend googling him unless you're into songs about pirates and cheeseburgers by an old man in a Hawaiian shirt. I sang along with Dad, about sunshine and parrots and 'Margaritaville'. It made me happy.

Sophie got home not long after we did, and the sky got a little more cloudy. 'Want a Tim Tam?' I asked, offering her the packet. She was stalking about like a grumpy gazelle, muttering about uni and Pilates and somebody called Mason. She ignored me, but I kept trying because I was on a Jimmy-Buffett-and-Tim-Tam high. 'I've discovered that if you dunk them in Nutella, they're *even more* the best food on the planet.'

Sophie shook her head fiercely. 'No. Weren't you listening? Pilates was cancelled, because Mason's obviously too busy with . . . I don't know. Whatever. I don't care. But no Pilates, no Tim Tam.'

'No Tim Tam, no meaning to life,' I said.

Sophie slumped onto one of the stools by the kitchen bench. 'I wish I could be like you sometimes,' she sighed.

'What?' I took the carton of milk from Dad's hand. It was time for Tim Tam Slams.

'English breakfast for me?' he said.

'Oh, Dad,' I sighed disparagingly. 'You can't slam a Tam in *tea*. It's Milo or nada.'

Dad laughed. 'Doctor Crozier would have my guts for garters if he knew, but okay, you've twisted my arm.'

I turned back to Sophie. 'Me?' I said. 'Why would you want to be like me? You're crazycakes, sis. Aside from my impeccable Tim-Tam-Slamming abilities, you're the winner in the Awesome at Life competition.'

Sophie puffed out her cheeks. 'I wish I was like you, because . . . I could never eat half a packet of Tim Tams. I'd want to kill myself if I did.'

I looked down at the biscuit packet in my hand. *Half a packet?* I'd eaten two. That's a regular serving size. But Sophie always had a talent for exaggerating.

'That's why you look like Natalie Portman, and I don't,' I said and shrugged.

Sophie hopped off the stool and grabbed her laptop bag. 'You look like how Clementine is meant to look. And I . . .' She shook her head. 'Who knows?'

'What are you on about?' I asked. Sophie shrugged and headed for the hallway door.

'I'll let you know when dinner's ready,' Dad called after her. 'Your mum's not home 'til later, so it's just the crack team tonight.'

Mum's a lawyer, Ms Hiller. I'm sure you knew that already, though; she's pretty well known around town. She's not home an awful lot, but that's okay, because Dad is, and Mum's here when she needs to be, and when she's not we know she's off being superwoman to people who need her more than we do.

'Crack team?' Dad tried again as Sophie kept walking. 'Crack team and your old dad's Spaghetti Bolo-crazy?'

She was gone. I looked at Dad and smiled ruefully.

'I'll just put on some more Jimmy,' Dad said. 'It helps me work through the pain.'

'Don't worry, Dad. I love your spag bol,' I said, kissing him on the cheek.

I went up to my room with my Milo and another bickie. I called hello to Fergus on the way, but he didn't reply.

I stood at his door for a moment, a fist hovering in the air and my stomach twisting in the usual uncertain way it did when I thought too hard about my brother. I felt angry and sad and guilty all at once, and in the end I didn't knock. I only pressed my palm to his door and wondered if he could somehow feel me there.

I sat on my bed and pulled out my English text, but I couldn't concentrate. I read the same paragraph over and over.

I couldn't stop thinking about the new boy.

He still intrigued me.

And the more I thought about him, the more I felt inspired.

I put down my novel and opened my notebook. I needed to get lost in the spaces between the words. I needed them to drag me down the rabbit hole.

That sounded a bit odd, didn't it?

It's only . . . when I write, I *know*. When I write, I feel as if I'm being pulled in the right direction. When I write, I don't worry about Fergus or the strange feelings I sometimes have about Cleo and Chelsea-Grace.

I don't worry at all. I let my fingers rest on the keys. And then I get carried away.

Did you see me?
Running, running.
Circles of time and mind and
beating feet and grass blades
flattening.
I saw you,
the sky empty in front of you, and
you were different.
Did you see me?
Standing, watching.
Did I pierce a hole in your sky?
Did you think, 'Who is she?'
like I thought,
'Who is he?'

Jeepers. I know. I know it's not any good. I'm tearing it out now and I'm putting it in the box below my bed. I don't let *anyone* read my poems.

Why would I let *you*?

Cleo kissed Todd Campbell.

That's the big news of the day, Ms Hiller.

She's been wanting to do it for ages. Todd's popular and good-looking and he wears the right clothes. He's friends with Sam Peterswalds from Grade 10, and for some reason that matters.

I've had to listen to Cleo talking about Todd for months, dissecting his every word and move and gesture.

And, finally, she kissed him. In the walkway between A Block and B Block. At morning break.

He was playing hackey sack with Sam, and Cleo was walking past, trying to look *alluring*, and Sam caught her by the arm and said, 'Cammo wants to kiss you.'

Cleo turned to Todd and, slowly, taking the time to puff out her lips a bit and tuck her blonde hair behind her ear to make him *wait*, which she says drives 'them' *crazy*, said, 'Is that true?'

And Todd said, 'Yes.' And so they kissed. Right in front of Sam and his girlfriend, Chenoa, and everybody else in the walkway.

'Are you going out now?' I asked her.

Cleo shrugged.

'I don't know. We're hanging out on Friday night, but it's a group thing. Sam and Chenoa are coming, and Brent, and I thought I might ask Chelsea-Grace to come, too.'

She must have noticed the look on my face, because she said, 'Sorry, Clem. It's just we thought it might be cool if Brent and Chels got together. It was Sam's idea. He's always teasing Brent about being a loser who doesn't have a girlfriend. It's hilarious. Anyway, it would be weird if you came too because it would be three couples and you. But I have an idea! On Friday I'll ask the guys if they have any *other* friends we can set you up with! There are so many hot guys in that group, and I know *some* of them are single. Don't worry, Clem. I'll arrange it all. And, in the meantime, we can catch up Saturday, right? Have some 3CD time?'

3CD is us, Ms Hiller. Me, Chels and Cleo.

We've been best mates since Grade 7. When our home group teacher, Ms Newman, called the roll, we realised the three of us had the initials CD – Clementine Darcy, Chelsea-Grace Darvell and Cleo Diaz.

This was back when Cleo still had braces and frizzy brown hair and hadn't yet discovered the modern miracle of tan-in-a-can. It was back when Chelsea-Grace was skinny and flat-chested, wearing glasses rather than contact lenses and dressing like she was still in primary school, in party dresses her mum picked out for her at Kmart. They didn't mind that I was a bit on the plump side. I didn't stand out, back then.

It feels wrong to admit it, but since Cleo dyed her hair blonde and had her braces taken off, and Chelsea-Grace grew curves, I don't *fit* with them like I used to.

I know they wish I was like them, so I wouldn't stick out, and they wouldn't need to worry about what other people thought of me all the time.

I wish – sometimes – that I had other friends; friends who'd like me just as I am. But I'd miss Chels and Cleo. I've been part of 3CD for so long, I can't imagine being out of it. I'd feel untethered. As if I was going to float away.

I wish that things could be like they were. Even a year ago, I was so certain we would be best friends until the end of time, but we seem so different now.

I can't help wondering . . .

What will it be like when one of them gets a proper boyfriend?

Or has *sex*?

Will it be so easy for us to be friends then?

Something tells me that when one friend has sex and the rest don't, things change. And when two friends have sex and one doesn't, everything changes. I know I'll be the last of 3CD to have sex. I'm not ready to do it yet. And it's not because I'm insecure, and it's not because I'm religious, or because I think it's morally *wrong* to have sex at our age.

I know I'll change my mind when I fall in love. I even wrote a poem about it. It's called 'When'. I'm putting it in here, but just for now. I'll rip it out later . . .

They say you know
'when'.
When it's love.
When it's right.
Your hand fits theirs
like puzzle pieces connecting –
two pieces of wide blue sky
with matching edges.
And everything that's big and wide and
frightening
in the world is squeezed between
your hand and his,
into nothing.

When somebody feels that way about me, and when I feel that way about them, I know I won't even have to think about it. It will *feel right*.

I haven't even kissed a boy yet. I'd like to. I'd like a kiss, with a boy who sees me the way I am. And likes me.

A Member of My Family by Clementine Darcy

My sister, Sophie Margaret Barbara Darcy, is perfect.

Her hair is just like the hair in shampoo ads: all swishy, as if it's made from dark satin. Her eyes are huge and her nose is small and elegant and her teeth are blindingly white and as straight as fence palings. She has clear, smooth olive skin. Her waist is tiny. She has never been bigger than a size eight. Ever.

Sophie is clever, too. I know I'm not *stupid*, but I am good at some things and rubbish at others. For instance, I do well at English and art, but put a quadratic equation in front of me and I hyperventilate.

Sophie, though, is every bit as clever at English as she is at science, *and* she can draw and play the flute. Oh, and she's good at sport, too. She plays netball and hockey *and* she does Pilates.

She's ridiculously bendy. To top it off, Soph is also a perfectly nice person. She's generous and funny and sensitive. She is, basically, the best person in the whole world.

Except that she's a bit grumpy lately. But I'm sure that will pass.

Once, Fergus asked if I minded having Soph as my sister. I knew what he meant. I knew he was asking if I minded being 'the other sister'; the one who wasn't Sophie. The chubby one. The ordinary one. The one who would always be okay, but never brilliant.

I said I didn't mind, and it was true. I'm lucky to have Sophie. Cleo's little sister is a right beast.

Sophie might be snappish at the moment, but she's stressed, that's all. Starting university must just be really full-on.

I asked Fergus if *he* minded having a sister like Sophie, and he said it was easier for him because he's a boy. I elaborated that it was easy for him because he's nothing like Soph in any way, not just gender. Fergus looks so different from both of us, with his blond hair, blue eyes and pale skin, whereas I'm brown-haired and olive-skinned like Soph.

'Plus, you've never cared much about school,' I pointed out, knowing Fergus wouldn't be offended. He's said as much himself, many times. It's just a fact. 'Nobody could compare *you* with our glorious sister.'

'Nobody is like Sophie,' he replied. 'She's the one person in the world who never has to try.'

'Oh, I don't know,' I joked. 'She does spend forever in the bathroom of a morning.'

'Yeah, and she looks just as pretty when she goes in as when she comes out,' he said. 'All that make-up rubbish is only for kicks. She's just . . . a natural. She's got it easy.'

I agreed with him, even though at the time it seemed as if Fergus didn't have to try, either. He had a lovely girlfriend called Alyssa, and he had a good job, working as a sous-chef. Maybe he did have it easy, back then. Maybe that's why, later, when things went bad, he found it so hard.

My Best Friend
by Clementine Darcy

That's a difficult one, Ms Hiller! Does it have to be *friend*, singular? Because if so, I truly can't do it. Chelsea-Grace and Cleo are my equal best friends. I can't disentangle them. They're woven together.

I hardly ever see them separately. They do, sometimes, spend time without me, but that's usually because I can't face going all the way to Hobart to see a gig by a pop singer I don't even like, or shopping for clothes I don't need. Sometimes I pull out of sleepovers, too, when I just don't feel like it. But otherwise, it's the three of us. 3CD. I can't choose one over the other.

So, my best *friends* are Cleo Diaz and Chelsea-Grace Darvell.

Before I met them, in primary school, my best friend was Leah Parker. She dropped me, though, at the beginning of Grade 6, because she wanted to join 'the Gang'.

Don't worry, Ms Hiller. They weren't a proper gang. There were no guns or graffiti or drugs involved. We were eleven years old!

The Gang was a clique of the coolest kids at Cooee Primary. Their leader was a girl called Angela, and the deputy was Diarne, and they both had *boyfriends*. They knew all the Beyoncé dance moves, and were allowed to go into the city by themselves at weekends wearing midriff tops and cut-off shorts, and they both had iPods. That was a big deal at the time.

Narelle was in the Gang, too. She and Leah were sort-of friends until, during the summer after Grade 5, their families went on holidays together to Bicheno. While they were there, Narelle invited Leah to join the Gang. Not me. Just Leah. And Leah joined.

She didn't even talk to me about it. On the first day of school she sat with me in Mr Dineen's class. The next day she moved tables and sat with the Gang girls. And when I asked her why she didn't want to sit with me anymore, she shrugged and said, 'Because you're just not pretty enough to be in the Gang, and you don't know music and stuff. You'll get over it.'

That day after school, Fergus found me crying into my pillow. He had just started Grade 10, and he was one of the most popular boys at Burnie High. Half the girls at Cooee Primary swooned when he dropped me at school every morning. *Everyone* loved Fergus.

He perched on my bed. 'What happened?'

I sat up, wiping away the tears. 'Leah doesn't like me anymore, and the Gang sang about me not having any friends, and I'm not pretty and don't know music.'

Fergus rolled his eyes. 'You know, Clem, we could totally get even. We could get angry, and I could help you make those stupid girls feel small and worthless. I'm popular. I have *the power*. But you know they're wrong, right, about you not being pretty?'

I shrugged. 'I don't know if I'm pretty. I'm not pretty like they are. But I think the way I look is fine.'

'The way you look is awesome,' Fergus corrected. 'So long as you know that, and that the way you are inside is awesome, too, and that we could get angry and get our revenge but we're better than that . . . I think the best thing to do would just be to listen to the music you like and dance like an idiot and forget it ever happened and go back to school tomorrow with your head held high and ignore them, because you're way too cool to take anything those girls say seriously. Deal?'

'Deal,' I said, smiling.

'So what music should we put on?' asked Fergus.

I grinned. 'I think we should put on the most *uncool* music in the world. We should put on Jimmy Buffett!'

When Dad found us dancing like lunatics around the lounge room to 'Cheeseburger in Paradise', he looked confused for a moment before shrugging and joining in. After a while, he did ask why we were dancing to his favourite crazy pirate music. 'Because it's uncool!' I cried out gleefully.

'Off to the orphanage with you!' Dad yelled, but he was laughing. We were all laughing. And Leah Parker was forgotten. And the next day I did go to school with my head held high. Because my big brother told me to, and he was the best person in the whole world.

I still see Leah around town sometimes. She went to Parklands High with the other Gang girls, while I went to Burnie High, like Sophie and Fergus. She pretends she doesn't know me. Which doesn't bother me at all. I'm channelling Jimmy Buffett when it comes to Leah. I'm breathing in and breathing out and moving on.

It feels like Chelsea-Grace and Cleo and I have been together forever, even though really it's only been a couple of years. And even though they've changed a lot and I haven't changed much at all, we're still 3CD. They're still my best friends.

Chelsea-Grace is a sweetie, really. Or at least she tries to be. She might open her mouth without thinking a lot, but she means well.

Chelsea-Grace doesn't like school much, but she's great at art. I'm always telling her she could make a career of it, if she would only try. I'm not sure Chelsea-Grace wants a career, though. All she thinks about are boys and babies. In her family, none of the women work. Her oldest sister, Caitlin, has three kids and her nineteen-year-old sister, Amy, just had a baby. As for her parents, they're *traditional.* They expect Chels to get married and have kids, not be an artist.

Cleo's a different kettle of fish entirely. She's extremely clever; she gets brilliant marks without even trying. She used to be proud of it, but now she seems embarrassed. She doesn't talk like a walking dictionary anymore and she only tells stories about Todd Campbell, not Alexander the Great or Einstein. At speech nights she rolls her eyes and yawns when she accepts her awards, and everyone laughs.

Cleo used to want to be a historian, but lately she's been reconsidering. It would mean moving Hobart to study, and she's not sure she wants to do that. She's thinking of enrolling in a child-care course instead, because you can do that in Burnie.

I hope she changes her mind. I think Cleo would be a terrible child-care worker. She doesn't have the patience. She's too blunt and unsympathetic. Also, I hope she finds the courage to leave Burnie, at least for a little while.

I wonder what will happen to 3CD after high school. I definitely don't want to stay in Wynyard. I want to study, maybe poetry. I know I could stay here, do some of my subjects at Burnie Uni and the rest online, like Soph does. But I want to see what it's like to live somewhere else, for a while – maybe even the UK. I could eat mushy peas, drink cider, picnic on Hampstead Heath . . . do a poetry workshop at Keats House and visit the graves of Chaucer and Tennyson and Robert Browning at Westminster Abbey. I could wander the Yorkshire moors, moody and full of important ideas . . .

I want to escape, Ms Hiller, to somewhere *other*. A new life, a new place, and . . .

Maybe even new friends. Does that make me horrible?

Sometimes, 3CD just feels like hard work. It feels as though if I were to do one tiny thing wrong we might fall apart.

I wish I didn't have to pretend with them. I wish 3CD could see right inside me – see the real Clementine – and like me as I am. I wish I could turn up to school dressed as a faerie or a pademelon and they'd *still* like me. But I think if I came to school dressed as a pademelon, they'd disown me forever.

So I'm finding myself hiding things. Like what's really going on with Fergus.

Chelsea-Grace and Cleo are my best friends, Ms Hiller. And I love them. But sometimes I feel as if life might be more of an adventure without them.

Then I imagine my world without them in it. And I feel very small and very scared.

'Finish this sentence,' you said. 'Life's too short not to . . .'

'Fight,' Gemma Gleave said, loudly. 'Fight against injustice. Fight against oppression. Fight against—'

'*Write* it,' you said, a half-smile on your face. '*Write* your ending to the sentence. If you can't think of an ending straight away, write until you come to it. It doesn't matter how long it takes, so long as you get there.'

Gemma began scribbling madly, a furious expression on her face. She's filled three pages already. Every so often, she pauses in her writing and checks her phone. Whoever is sending her messages makes the anger melt, and she smiles before returning to her writing and her rage.

I don't know much about Gemma Gleave: only that she's vegetarian, and sometimes she talks in class about wars I didn't know were being fought. But she's popular, too. I wonder how she does that; how she manages to stay popular while having opinions.

While being *herself.*

Life's too short not to . . .

I wish I knew the answer straight away, Ms Hiller, but I don't. I wish I spent my weekend doing all the things people promise themselves they'll do before they die. I didn't. My weekend was nice – some of it – but it was hardly an adventure.

My crazy, thrilling weekend began on the couch, watching television with my dad because I had nowhere to go. It was Friday night. Cleo and Chelsea-Grace were on their double date. Soph was out. Mum was working. I tried to lure Fergus out of his room to watch TV with us, but when I knocked and went in he pulled the doona over his head and turned away. I noticed some empty plates on the floor and picked them up. As I left, I heard him say, 'You don't need to do that, Clem. I can do that.'

I went to bed early and woke up feeling sad.

On Saturday morning Cleo called, and she was gushing with excitement because Todd had asked her to be his girlfriend. I asked about Chelsea-Grace and Brent, and Cleo laughed and said, 'You have to come over, Clem. It's wicked.'

When I arrived at Cleo's house, Chels was sitting on Cleo's bed, still in her pyjamas. She must have stayed over.

I was all right with that.

She had that look on her face – the one she gets when she has a secret she can't wait to tell, but she's going to pretend as if there's nothing going on until you beg her to spill everything.

'Is it about Brent?' I asked, dropping my overnight bag on the floor.

3CD often stay at each other's houses, sometimes for days at a time. Usually it's Cleo's place. It used to be mine more, but because of what's going on with Fergus I don't really like them being there anymore.

It makes it easier to pretend the whole Fergus thing isn't happening.

Chelsea-Grace shook her head quickly. She hugged her knees to her chest and leaned her chin on them.

She was blushing.

'Just tell her, Chelsea-Grace!' Cleo flopped onto the bed.

I looked at my best friends. They were so *right* together, snuggled up on Cleo's glittery bedspread. I felt so far away from them, sitting on the beanbag.

'What?' I tried to sound excited, even though my stomach was tying in knots.

'Chelsea-Grace kissed Sam!' Cleo squealed.

Chelsea-Grace shook her head, her rosy pink cheeks turning a darker shade of red. 'Hon!' she scolded, grinning from ear to ear.

'But he's going out with Chenoa!' I still felt funny in my stomach.

'I know.' Chelsea-Grace shrugged.

'Are they breaking up?' I asked.

'I don't think so,' said Chelsea-Grace. 'Maybe. Oh no! Hon. You don't think I did the wrong thing, do you?'

'I don't think . . .' I didn't finish my sentence. I didn't know what to say that wouldn't have sounded naive, and plus, Chelsea-Grace seemed so happy. 'Does Chenoa know?' I asked.

'I don't think so,' she said. 'It happened after she went home. She had cramps. She was being a real grump all night, wasn't she, Cleo?'

'Horrendous,' Cleo agreed. 'I don't know why he puts up with her.'

'And Brent was being annoying.' Chelsea-Grace grimaced. 'I mean, I'm not trying to be nasty, but he kept talking about really boring stuff.'

'What boring stuff?' I asked. I've always thought Brent seems nice.

Chelsea-Grace shrugged. 'He's . . . I'm not trying to be mean, but Brent isn't anywhere near as, you know, what's the word?' Chels looked at Cleo for assistance.

'Charismatic?' Cleo offered.

Chels nodded vigorously. 'That's so the word I was after! Thanks, hon. Anyway, it's true. I'm only being honest. He's *not* as charismatic as Sam. Sam's mature. He's in Grade 10, and he's old for Grade 10, too, because he came from Queensland, remember? So he's, like, seventeen?'

And yet he still hangs out with Grade 9s, I wanted to say. I've always thought it odd that Sam's best mates are both a grade below him, and so is his girlfriend. He acts as if he's king of them all.

But maybe it doesn't mean anything. Maybe it simply means Sam doesn't care how old people are – that he likes them based on who they are. Which is a nice way to be, I suppose.

'He's got his P-plates and everything,' Chelsea-Grace went on happily. 'Whereas little Brent, he's so . . . fifteen. And he kind of has bad skin too, poor thing.'

'But that doesn't make him boring,' I protested. 'Bad skin doesn't make you boring.' I didn't even get started on the fact that Brent isn't at all little. He's the ruckman for the under-18s! He's *tall.*

Chels wrinkled up her nose. 'I know. It wasn't that. It was . . . I'm usually good at listening to boys talk, and pretending they're being interesting when they're not. But I have to be *into* them to do that. And I didn't feel it with Brent, you know? He kept talking about his little sister and how she won some prize at school, and you *know* how much I like kids, but his sister's, like, eleven, which isn't exactly cute anymore. So when Sam said he needed to go outside for a ciggie, I said I needed one too, just so I could get away from Brent—'

'But you don't smoke!' I interrupted.

'I do, socially!' Chelsea-Grace raised her chin in the air, as if she was daring me to disagree. I didn't say anything. 'So, once we were outside, Sam was pacing and shaking his head, and I put my hand on his arm—'

'You didn't tell me that!' Cleo said, and I felt secretly glad for a moment that Cleo didn't already know everything.

'I forgot, hon. I'm sorry.' Chelsea-Grace bit her lip. 'Don't be mad at me? Anyway, then he turned to me and said, *I'm sorry if you've had a bad night because of Chenoa's mood*, and I said it wasn't his fault, and then he asked if I liked Brent, and I said not really, and he said that Brent's a good bloke but he's useless with women. I think I laughed at that. I don't remember. I didn't want to say anything nasty. Anyway, the next thing I know he's brushing the hair out of my eyes and saying that what he likes – *likes* – about me is that I'm easy-going and sweet, not like Chenoa. And then he kissed me. And that's it. It was . . . I can't explain it, Clem. It was so *sexy*. Then he pulled back and looked like he was going to say something, but suddenly Brent came outside, because he felt weird being inside with Cleo and Todd, and so, well, that was that.'

'Are you going to see him again?' I asked.

'Well, *I* don't know!' Chels spread her arms wide in front of her. 'It's a complicated situation.'

'I hope you do,' said Cleo. 'Then we can double date. Hey! Maybe we can get Brent together with Clem! That would be wicked! I talked to Todd about the other guys in the group, and there are a few possibilities, but Brent is third-in-command, isn't he? After Sam and Todd? So it would be amazing if he and Clemmie got together, wouldn't it?'

'Yes!' Chels cried. 'And that would be nice for him, too! I think he's sad about not hooking up with me. Poor thing. Do you think you'd like to go out with him, Clem?' Chels looked at my face, searching. 'It would be great if you could. If 3CD could, like, do stuff together, with the boys. That would be cool.'

I shrugged. I barely knew 'the boys'. I certainly wasn't sure if I wanted to go out with one of them.

'We have to get rid of Chenoa first,' said Cleo.

'Oh! Exactly!' Chelsea-Grace cried. 'How will we do it?'

'Well, first we could . . .'

I tuned out, after a while. Listening to my friends plotting the demise of Sam and Chenoa just seemed . . . *grubby*. So while they planned and schemed, I let my thoughts drift. They floated between how much I felt like a glass of juice . . . and how much I *hated* the crappy R'n'B song Chels had put on . . . and Fergus . . . and, eventually, the boy under the cider gum.

I started making up a little poem in my head.

Blackcurrant juice and
boys in tweed waistcoats.
Songs about nothing at all.
Heads full of somethings,
bouncing, colliding,
trying so hard not
to fall.

'Did you hear me?' Cleo leapt off the bed and kneeled in front of me.

'What?'

'Sam texted Chelsea-Grace!' She held up Chelsea-Grace's phone as evidence. 'He asked if she wants to catch a movie on Friday, and Chels didn't want to seem too keen so she texted back to say yes but not this Friday – next Friday. And only if she could bring *you*, and if Sam would ask Brent to be your date. Sam said he'd ask. It's so exciting – a 3CD classic moment! Why weren't you listening?'

'What about Chenoa?' I asked, feeling like a broken record.

'Sam didn't mention her.' Chels looked slightly annoyed. 'Cleo, can we watch a movie? I don't want to talk anymore. It's making me stressed.'

♡

During the movie (*Mean Girls* – again), Chelsea-Grace fell asleep, and Cleo whispered to me that I didn't need to be nervous about Todd and Brent and Sam. I said that I wasn't. Cleo looked confused.

'Oh, I thought you would be. They're just so hot, and everyone wants to be with them. Don't be worried, though, Clem. We'll be there with you.'

Holy Cheezels. I *hadn't* been worried, but after that I somehow started to be. I didn't know what to say, so I turned back to the movie.

After a while, Cleo leaned in again. 'I really like Todd,' she whispered. 'I think I'm going to have sex with him.'

I just nodded.

Later, we went shopping. Sam had confirmed Brent was in for next Friday night, and the girls wanted new outfits. By now I felt sick, to be honest. Something about all of this didn't feel *right*.

Cleo picked out a blue singlet with sparkly butterflies on it, and a pair of tight black jeans. Chelsea-Grace found a low-cut floral bandage dress that made her look even curvier.

'Are you going to buy something?' she asked as we walked through the arcade.

'I think I'll wear my shirt dress,' I said. 'The grey one?'

'Isn't that a bit, like, plain?' asked Chelsea-Grace. 'No offence, hon. I just want you to look pretty.'

And so I couldn't escape it. The girls dragged me around and made me try on clothes that would never fit.

'Wrong size,' I called out for the millionth time.

'I thought you were a fourteen?' Cleo said.

'I am.' I tried not to feel annoyed. 'These must be small fourteens.'

'There really should be a rule that clothes sizes have to be the same in every shop,' said Cleo, but she didn't sound convinced.

In the end, I grabbed a size-sixteen dress off a rack while the others weren't looking. It was black and made from stiff, slimming fabric. It had a deep V-neck, which would show off my cleavage, and a flare at the hips, which Chelsea-Grace's magazines say is flattering. I thought I might buy some patterned stockings to go with it.

'I'll try this one on,' I called to the girls, who were looking at scarves.

I undressed in the change room. I examined myself in the full-length mirror, from every angle, and I was pleased with what I saw. I may be bigger than the other girls, but I'm toned. I don't have cellulite, and I have nice boobs. I have long legs, too. Sophie says she's jealous of my legs. She's shorter than I am and says that's why she has to watch what she eats. 'If I put on a kilo, it looks like five,' she grumbles. 'And if I eat one chocolate too many, it puts on a kilo. It's so unfair.'

It's not true at all, Ms Hiller.

I don't know why Sophie's so finicky about food. But she's that way about so many things. She's a perfectionist and a creature of habit. She always puts mascara on her left eye and then her right, and she only ever uses Smiggle highlighters for her exam study.

When we were younger she'd only eat her dinner off a certain plate, with a green trim around the edge; if she couldn't eat off that plate, she'd cry and refuse to eat at all.

Come to think of it, she's become even more picky since Fergus went to his room.

I've never been tempted to diet. I let my eyes scan my body in the change-room mirror. I'm not fat. I might say I am, sometimes, but I don't ever mean it. Compared with Sophie, or anyone in Hollywood or on catwalks, I *am* big, but it's all relative.

I swivelled from side to side. I might not look like a gym bunny, but the parts that jiggle are the ones that are *meant* to jiggle. Because I'm a girl.

I slithered into the slinky dress. It fit me perfectly.

'Is *this* one okay?' Cleo called out. I could hear exasperation in her voice. I pulled back the curtain. Cleo's eyebrows rose. 'You look great, Clem. Classic.'

Later, we went to Banjo's for afternoon tea. Chelsea-Grace had a chicken salad. Cleo ordered a Diet Sprite. I had scones with jam and cream. Because I *wanted* to. Life's too short not to have scones occasionally.

Hi, Ms Hiller.

I am going to sticky-tape in here a poem I wrote last night. Two poems, actually – an old one first, and then a new one.

Initially, like I always do, I put the new poem in the box beneath my bed. But then I took it out again. I can't explain, Ms Hiller. I don't know why I want you to see it. I might change my mind. I might unstick it and return it to the box. I've never showed anyone one of my poems before, let alone two.

And I've been writing all my life.

Before I knew how to form letters, I'd draw series of pictures, like comics, and tell the stories of them out loud – three-year-old tales about our cat, Izzy, or our neighbour with the mole on her cheek shaped like a fish.

The first time I can remember writing a poem, it was about me and Fergus, inspired by a Les Murray poem I fell in love with after Dad took me to hear him speak one time.

They're talking about it, all over Wynyard,
at the wharf and the Chinese restaurant,
on the beach and by the pond where the ducks eat bread,
they're whispering and pointing,
and, from the bakery, people creep, jelly slices in hand,
to see it:
My brother is skating down Goldie Street,
where he shouldn't, where nobody else does, where the signs forbid.
They can't stop him.

And while they all gasp and hold their hands over their mouths,
I think, That's my brother. And he's not skating. He's flying.
I watch him whoosh past and disappear up Church Street.

Don't worry, Ms Hiller, my poetry has improved since then.

I hope.

But it's not bad for a ten-year-old, right?

Last night, I said 'hello' to Sophie and she didn't reply. And suddenly, I got angry.

'Good golly. That's just what I need – another sibling who doesn't talk to me,' I yelled.

Sophie jumped. 'What? What the hell, Clementine?' She looked up at me, and her glazed eyes began to blaze. 'I've got an idea,' she snapped. 'Why don't you just shut up and stop feeling sorry for yourself?'

She had all her textbooks in front of her. I realised she'd been concentrating hard and hadn't heard me when I first said hello. But I was still angry. She is always in such a foul mood lately.

'What is up your *bum*, sourpuss?' I asked.

'Oh, you know, it's called being an *adult* and having *adult* problems to deal with, Clementine,' she said. She only uses my full name when she's really angry.

'HAH!' I cried. 'What problems have you got? You're beautiful and smart and *perfect*!' I basically spat out the last word.

'Yeah, *right*.' She leapt up, knocking her chair to the floor behind her, and I noticed that her jeans were baggy. Her wrists were so pale and fragile, I could see veins through her skin. Her face was grey, and there were bags under her eyes.

She looked sick. And I wondered if maybe she had looked like that for a while, and I hadn't noticed. Or hadn't wanted to.

'I'm *perfect*,' she spat. 'I never have any problems. I never mess up. I never, ever, ever do anything wrong, and that's the way this family likes me, right? Because they've already got crazy Fergus and naive, dreamy Clementine to deal with. How lucky they are that good old Sophie never causes any TROUBLE.'

She tore from the room, and I stood there watching the space she'd left behind, wondering where my sister had disappeared to.

It's not only her body that is shrinking. The Sophie I knew seems to be fading away.

We were the best of friends, once. She never used to snap at me.

And she used to smile sometimes.

She and Fergus were the most amazing brother and sister a girl could ask for, and now Fergus won't talk to any of us, and when Sophie does talk it's only to spit venom.

And does she really think I am *naive*?

I was hurt and confused, Ms H, and I thought, for a moment, I might call Cleo or Chels and pour my heart out to them. But I knew they wouldn't understand.

So I grabbed an apricot from the fruit bowl, and I opened my favourite purple notebook, the one that Fergus bought me, and I wrote a poem instead.

Sophie,
all angles,
turns sideways,
disappears.

Sophie,
apples,
diet cola,
lettuce,
hollow cheeks,
eyes like unfilled wells.
Sophie,
hard,
brittle,
crackling.
Sophie
holds one edge
of a rubber band.
I hold
the other.
We're both pulling.
I know
it will snap.

What do you think, Ms Hiller?

Are you going to read this, Ms Hiller?

Is anybody listening?

The Thing I Am Most Scared Of by Clementine Darcy

The thing I'm most scared of is death.

I think people are silly when they say they're scared of other things – spiders, snakes, bungee jumping . . . They're missing the big picture. They are frightened of spiders, snakes and bungee jumping because they are worried those things will kill them.

I'm not religious, so I don't believe I'm going somewhere when I die, like heaven or nirvana, but I do think maybe your spirit lingers somehow. Maybe as a ghost. Or an *essence*. An echo of you.

I hope that's true. Not for me in particular; more for the people I love. If Fergus died . . .

I don't want to think about Fergus dying.

Cleo believes that death is oblivion. She argues that it doesn't scare her because, when she's dead, she won't know it. That thought *does* scare me. The not knowing. The not existing. The *nothing*. I can't think of anything more terrifying than not *being*.

Once, I asked Fergus what he was most afraid of. We'd just watched a Japanese horror movie, and it scared the living daylights out of me, but Fergus laughed the whole way through.

This was *before*, of course.

'Aren't you scared of anything?' I asked.

'No,' Fergus said.

Just like that. Straight away. Certain. 'No.'

I challenged him. 'Not of death? Not spiders? Clowns? I heard some people are scared of peanut butter. You're *truly* scared of nothing?'

The smile slid from his face. He was serious now. 'Yeah, nothing. Nothing scares me.'

Sometimes I sit outside Fergus's door. I don't knock. I don't call out. I just sit there and listen for his breathing.

Maybe my own death isn't what I'm most afraid of, Ms Hiller.

I saw the boy again today.

He was in the covered way leading to the canteen. He wasn't wearing the Sherlock cap this time – he had on a peculiar round little hat, a black one with a curly brim. I think they're called pork-pie hats, though to me they look more like Wagon Wheels.

He also sported a black pinstripe suit: waistcoat, vest complete with fob watch, and tapered pants. A burgundy cravat wrapped around his neck.

He looked completely crazycakes.

I couldn't stop staring.

Compared to all the other boys, who were dressed like they'd stepped out of a boy-band video clip or a Just Jeans catalogue, he was so . . . unexpected.

He smiled at me again.

In the split second before he passed me. And he had dimples.

I gazed after his retreating back. He took a left and disappeared down the stairs leading to the art and drama rooms. I wonder what he was doing down there at lunchtime . . .

I only ever spend my breaks in the lunch room near the canteen. I could go anywhere else in the school, but I always go to the lunch room. I sit with Cleo and Chelsea-Grace, and Rosalinde Crowley, who is Chelsea-Grace's cousin, and Kristie Redfern, who does dancing with Cleo, and Kristie's friend Rachael, and Melanie and Melissa (the Mels), who are best friends and who Chelsea-Grace knows from primary school.

That's our table. Every lunchtime. And we . . . what do we do? We talk. And sometimes play cards. Occasionally, some of the boys from Sam's table come over and play cards with us. And I eat lunch, but some of the others don't sometimes, if they're on a diet.

Today I had a wonderful lunch – leftover ratatouille, with eggplant and ripe organic tomatoes, which Sophie made last night. She loves cooking, and she's brilliant at it, but she never eats her own creations.

I sat there wishing Sophie would eat her cooking. It might cheer her up if she ate some delicious ratatouille.

Meanwhile, Chelsea-Grace and Cleo were at the other end of the table, poring over an article in a glossy magazine. I was sitting next to Kristie, who was rabbiting on to Rachael about a movie she saw at the weekend. 'It was, like, foreign? *So* annoying. But the guys, ohmigod, so *hot*.'

The Mels were doing homework. They're always doing homework at lunchtime because they forget to do it the night before. Rosalinde was in the lunch queue.

I people-watched.

I watched Gemma Gleave talking animatedly to a girl with short spiky hair. She held her phone in one hand and a stack of pamphlets in the other. I couldn't see what they were for.

Clarissa Docklands was arguing with her boyfriend. She was red in the face. He looked bored.

Ioannis Poulos was strumming lightly on his guitar. There was a girl with her arm around him. A groupie, I guess. He has piles of them, but he never seems very interested. They hang off him and he lets them.

I think Ioannis is all right, but compared with the boy in the pork-pie hat, he's still ordinary. Turn on Rage any Saturday morning and you can see a hundred boys who look just like Ioannis, playing guitars and looking angst-ridden while singing about tortured love and dark moments of the soul. (Or, in Ioannis's case, chips and gravy. Ioannis is obsessed with chips and gravy. Even his love songs manage to feature chips and gravy.)

I've never seen another boy like the one in the pork-pie hat.

I know we have a topic today . . .

But something has happened. Something strange. Something even stranger than the last strange thing.

I need to write about the new strange thing, so I am wondering if I can do the topic tomorrow – swap days? Is that in the rules?

Are there any rules, Ms Hiller? I am looking at you quizzically. You don't seem to have noticed. You are reading a book called *Sophie's World*. I think my Sophie has read that one, Ms Hiller. She hardly ever reads books that aren't for school, so it must be good.

As we came into class today, you gave each of us a packet of Wizz Fizz sherbet. You said eating Wizz Fizz makes your brain switch on; makes you think of things outside the square. *Strange* things, you said.

Gryff snorted his Wizz Fizz but I ate mine, using the tiny plastic spade that comes in the packet. And now all I can think of is the *strange thing* that happened to me.

I spent my entire lunch hour with the boy.

Completely

by

accident.

I was walking back from English, where we'd had to give a speech on our favourite poet. It was difficult choosing between Sylvia and Les Murray and Donne, but in the end I went with Donne. I talked about his preoccupation with the idea that four 'humours' controlled the human body: phlegm, yellow bile, blood and black bile. He believed that having too much or too little of any one of these humours threw the body and soul out of whack.

As I walked towards the lunch room, I was thinking about Sophie and how lately it seems as though she has an excess of black bile – of melancholy . . .

Melancholy
is a packet of Tim Tams
opened
on the bench before you,
and you sitting,
staring,
but not touching,
your eyes full of—

That's as far as I got, Ms Hiller, because at that moment I tripped on a piece of curled-up carpet. My elbows hit the ground first. My chin wasn't far behind. My books spilled every which way, along with my phone, my wallet and seventeen thousand tampons.

I scrabbled to a crouching position and then overbalanced again.

Nobody bent to help me.

Some Grade 8 girls laughed at me.

Not one person asked if I was all right.

Are you thinking that this is when the boy appeared? A heroic knight on a white horse, sweeping in to rescue me?

That's not what happened, Ms Hiller.

After I fell over, I didn't feel like going to the lunch room. I was shaken, and peeved that those girls had laughed at me. I was feeling *choleric*, Ms Hiller.

I decided to take my lunch (leftover green curry and rice)

and my book and sit outside; let book-smell and sunbeams bring my humours back into balance.

I went to the edge of the sports field and up the hill, and I sat beneath the cider gum.

I curled up against the rough bark.

I liked the smell there. I liked the quiet.

I began to read, but after a few paragraphs I started to get that unsettled feeling: the one that comes when you know somebody is close by, but you can't *see* them. That odd, breath-catching, goosepimply feeling.

I got to my knees, peered around the side of the tree trunk . . . and found myself face to face with the boy, who was in the exact same position!

I burst out laughing. I knew how ridiculous we must look. The boy started laughing, too. Then there was an awkward moment where it was obvious neither of us knew whether we should go to our own side of the tree or sit together.

Finally the boy said, 'Join me? This side of the tree is much nicer.'

I sat beside him. I was so close I could have put my arm around him. If I'd wanted to.

'Hello, Clementine,' he said.

A shiver went up my spine. How did the boy know my name?

He must have noticed my surprise, because he nodded at my lunch box. Sure enough, there on my very old green Décor lunch box, in faded letters written years ago, was my name.

The boy smiled. He really does have a nice smile.

He was wearing a bowler hat, a leather vest, and funny half-length trousers that puffed at his thighs and cinched in tightly at his knees. *Knickerbockers.* His black lace-up boots went all the way up to their hems. The boy dipped his hand into the pocket of his leather vest, pulled out his fob watch and flicked it open and shut.

Open and shut.

Open and shut.

'I'm Fred,' he said, still flicking.

'Pleased to meet you, Fred,' I said, and cringed. I sounded so stilted and old-fashioned.

But then I had to laugh. Old-fashioned? I was talking to a boy with a fob watch and puffy pants!

'What's funny?' he asked, smiling that nice smile again. Deep in my belly, something jolted.

'N-nothing,' I stammered. A blush began to sneak up my neck. 'Nothing's funny, really. Um, you're new, aren't you? We don't get many new kids here. Are you . . . are you liking it?'

Fred nodded. 'It's different. Very, actually – we moved down from Sydney.' He smiled wryly. 'I do miss my favourite cupcake shop, and it's hard adjusting to being in a one-bookshop town – although Not Just Books is great. I might have to change classes soon, too; they still haven't finalised my schedule, which is a bit tiresome. But these are all minor quibbles in the scheme of things. At least compared with . . .'

Fred trailed off, suddenly looking pensive. I imagined cogs and wheels and pulleys and gaskets all popping and whirring inside the engine of his head, producing thoughts I was not privy to.

The silence stretched out between us. Fred didn't seem to mind it, but I started to feel uneasy. I noticed a notebook on his knee. It had a silver cover with an odd bubble-shaped airship embossed on it.

'What are you writing?' I asked.

'I'm not entirely certain,' said Fred, smiling. 'I mean, I know the basic premise and the setting, but apart from that it's in the hands of the gods. I'm sure once it works itself out, it will tell me.'

We sat in silence for another moment as I pondered the idea that a book might tell its author what it wanted to be, instead of the other way around. That's how I feel about my poetry, Ms Hiller – as though it takes me over. As though it's doing its own thing and I'm along for the ride.

'What do you have for lunch?' asked Fred, yanking me from my thoughts. He tipped his bowler hat at my lunch box.

'Green curry,' I replied. 'Soph made it. My sister. She's the second-best cook in our family, after Fergus of course, but he's not cooking at the moment. So Soph cooks, even though she hardly eats. Otherwise Dad takes charge, because Mum works crazy hours, whereas Dad works from home half the time, and besides, Mum could burn water. If Dad and Soph are busy, we usually get takeaway. Although sometimes I make pasta or jaffles, and I do extra for Fergus because he— Sorry, I'm babbling.'

Fred smiled. 'I think babble is a splendid word,' he said.

'Me, too!' I agreed. I felt all warm.

'Words are magic . . . transformative . . . *thaumaturgic.* Don't you think?' asked Fred.

I wasn't sure *what* I thought about that.

A breeze struck up, carrying the smell of cinnamon and milk from a small saucepan at Fred's feet. The saucepan had a silver spoon in it. 'What do you have? For lunch?' I asked Fred, pointing.

'I had porridge,' he answered.

'That's a strange thing to have for lunch,' I said. 'And, hold on, how did you even cook porridge at school?'

'There's a hob down in the art rooms.' Fred lifted a shoulder. 'By the graffiti wall. You know the one? Where the artistic types draw marvellous paintings and write words of wisdom. I like that wall, Clementine. I often think I'd like to write something there myself, one day. I simply haven't quite decided yet what I'd like to write. And also, I'm not sure I'm allowed. I don't think I'm arty enough. But I do sneakily use their hob. I think it's intended for some sort of creative purpose, but it's also very handy for heating one's *strange* lunch items.'

I bit my lip. 'Sorry for calling it strange,' I said. 'I shouldn't have called your lunch strange.'

'That's okay,' he said, smiling kindly. 'It *is* strange, I suppose. If you're from this era.' He fixed me steadily with his hazel eyes.

My stomach jumped again. It was not an unpleasant feeling.

'Aren't we all from the same era?' I asked, spearing a snow pea with my fork.

'From a biological viewpoint,' Fred answered. 'But, as human beings, we have developed a concept of free will, which extends to an ability to make decisions that set us on a particular life course of our choosing. This encompasses the era that we choose to mentally inhabit.'

'I'm not sure I quite got that,' I admitted.

Fred looked away, at the sports field and the gum trees and wattles that lined it. I watched his eyes follow a magpie as it flitted from tree to tree. Eventually, he turned back to me. 'Have you ever heard someone say they were born at the wrong time?' he asked.

I nodded. 'My dad says it about Sophie. He reckons she

should have been alive during the World Wars, because she's such a fusspot and so practical. He says she'd have made a good nurse for the soldiers. Sophie always says, *Thanks, Dad. So you'd have me shipped off to a battlefield and possibly blown up by the Germans. You must love me so very much.*'

Fred laughed. 'Your family sounds great.'

'I love them to bits.'

It was the truth, Ms Hiller.

Despite everything.

Then I said something more. I don't know why I said it, exactly; only that there was something in Fred's hazel eyes that *urged* me to. 'I really do love them,' I said, 'but I'm worried about my brother, because he won't come out of his room, and I'm worried about my sister, because she seems really stressed.'

After a pause, Fred said, 'Well, that's understandable. We always worry about the people we love, don't we? But if you're busy worrying about them, who's worrying about you?'

I shrugged. 'I don't think I need anyone to worry about me. I'm boring.'

Fred grinned. 'Oh, I don't think *that's* true.' He inclined his head. 'Do you ever feel as if you were born at the wrong time, Clementine Darcy?'

I thought for a moment. 'Sometimes,' I said, truthfully. 'I sometimes wonder why I had to be born in a time when there seems to be only one way for a woman to look beautiful, and it's not the way I look. But it's not only that. I don't care about so many of the things my friends care about. I'm not into gadgets. I'm more into the music my dad likes than what's popular – country and folk. I'm not into fashion. Is that what you mean?'

Fred nodded. 'Yes,' he said. 'That's exactly what I mean. I think we've lost some of the magic.'

'That's sad,' I said. 'I wonder if we can get the magic back.'

'Oh, there's still magic here.' Fred looked at me oddly when he said that. It felt as if he was staring right inside me – seeing all the bits I never show anyone.

Seeing *Clementine.*

I was overcome by a strong desire to change the subject. 'So, what are you reading?' I pointed to a thick, dog-eared novel sitting on the grass beside him.

He picked up the book and passed it to me.

The cover showed two shadowy figures inside an elaborate, Industrial Age-looking engine of some sort. My thoughts flicked back to Fred's brain – its cogs and wheels. I wondered if this was what it looked like inside.

'What's it about?' I asked.

'You should read it,' he said. 'I can't tell you what it's about. You have to form that impression yourself. Borrow it. I've got another copy, and I've read it before. It's only recent, but I believe it will come to be regarded as a seminal work in the steampunk canon, in years to come.'

'What's steampunk?' I asked.

Fred smiled, slowly – that same, quite lovely smile. 'It's the era I choose to live in,' he said.

The bell rang shrilly, signalling the end of the lunch break. Fred stood and extended his hand. He pulled me up as if I was made of air.

As we walked towards the classrooms, Fred said to me, 'Why doesn't your brother leave his room?'

'We don't . . . know,' I said slowly. 'One day he went in there and he didn't come back out.'

'Maybe he's building a time machine,' said Fred – and it's funny, because if somebody else had said that it would have sounded sarcastic, but when Fred said it, it seemed gentle. He was trying to cheer me up.

'I think maybe he'd like to do that,' I said. 'Some things went wrong for him. I think he would like to go back in time and fix them.'

Fred didn't say anything else until just before we got to A Block. 'I'm usually under the gum tree at lunchtime,' he said quietly. 'I nearly went into the lunch room on the first day, but it was somewhat overwhelming. I like the silence up there on the hill. If it's raining, I go to the art rooms. It's quiet there, too. So that's where you can find me, if you want to look.'

That was an invitation, right? He wouldn't have said it if he didn't *want* me to look? My heart did a little flutter around in my chest. Which is problematic, Ms Hiller, because wonderful as he may be, Fred is obviously a geek. He wears bowler hats and doesn't believe he lives in this era. He talks about things I've never heard of, and he eats porridge for lunch. Meaning . . .

Cleo and Chelsea-Grace definitely wouldn't approve.

They want me to go out with Brent. If I do that, 3CD will be close again. If I was to go out with Fred instead . . .

But why am I even thinking about going out with Fred? I only just met him! I don't know anything about him, apart from that he has dimples and deep hazel eyes and he likes porridge and tea and when he looks at me it's as if he can see everything.

That doesn't mean anything, does it? That's not enough for me to go all *peculiar* about?

I am going to read Fred's book. It's in front of me now.

My hand keeps drifting to the cover, and I like that Fred has turned down some of the pages' corners. I wonder if they're the important bits. I'm looking forward to reading those.

They might help me work things out.

My Favourite Meal by Clementine Darcy

My favourite meal happened a year ago. It was Fergus's birthday. He turned nineteen. He told us that he didn't want a party – he only wanted to be with his family, and he wanted to cook a meal for *us*, instead of the other way around.

I was happy Fergus wanted to be with us on his birthday. I was glad to know that, even though he was getting older, he wasn't leaving us quite yet.

Leaving me.

Sophie may be the perfect one, and I love her to bits and pieces, but Fergus was always my hero. Because while Sophie did everything perfectly, Fergus did everything *fearlessly*. And if he mucked up, he didn't *give* up. Instead, he waited until his wounds had healed and then he tried again.

Skateboarding? Fergus has a bench named after him, thanks to the head-shaped chunk he took out of it the day he decided to skate down Mount Street.

That's the steepest hill in Burnie.

Cooking? You should see all the scars Fergus has from burns and cuts. The supervising chef from his apprenticeship used to call him Bandaid because of his erratic skills with the kitchen knife. He worked on it, though, and now he could give Jamie Oliver a run for his money.

Playing the trumpet? In the beginning Dad invested in industrial-grade earplugs for the whole family. In time, though, with the help of his music teacher, Mr Zappa, Fergus got better. Never *great*, but better.

Love? Well . . .

Alyssa had an after-school job as a waitress at the restaurant where Fergus cooked. She is *beautiful*. Not that Fergus is ugly, but Alyssa's the sort of beautiful you expect to see paired up with the cricket captain, or the footy full-forward – not a laid-back, skateboarding chef. And she did turn him down the first hundred times he asked her out. But he kept on asking.

And she kept on saying no.

So Fergus found out what her favourite song, colour and movie were: 'You Are So Beautiful' by Joe Cocker, purple, and *Bridget Jones's Diary*. Then he dressed up like Mark Darcy from *Bridget Jones*, in a jumper with a reindeer on it, and he picked her some lavender from our neighbour's garden, and he went into the restaurant singing Joe Cocker, and *of course* she said yes *then*.

Fergus never gave up and, in the end, he got the job and the girl. Not by being perfect, but by working hard. And I loved him for that.

This is what Fergus cooked us on his birthday:

ENTRÉE

Chickpea and vegetable broth
Grilled octopus
Huon Valley mushroom risotto

MAIN

Moroccan chicken with preserved lemon and
butter couscous
Tasmanian Atlantic salmon
Grilled polenta with beetroot and orange ratatouille

DESSERT

Citrus pavlova with homemade pistachio ice-cream
Cardamom crème caramel
Caramelised pear tart with Chantilly cream

We all 'ordered' different meals so we could try some of everything. Even Sophie sampled every dish. Dad let me have champagne, too, and I had just enough that I felt boundless and free, and we all toasted Fergus and told him how wonderful and special he is.

It wasn't until right at the end of the night that Soph asked why Alyssa wasn't there.

Fergus went quiet then.

He went to his room.

And he hasn't come back to us.

Last night, I decided to try to spend some time with Soph.

She seemed down again when she came home from uni, and I was remembering what I'd said to Fred, about how much I love her.

I don't think I actually expected her to agree to hang out, but to my surprise, when I asked, she said, 'Study can wait. I'm way ahead. I can afford a night off.'

Mum and Dad were out to dinner with friends, on a rare night off work for Mum, so it was just the two of us. I cooked myself some grilled cheese on toast, and Soph made miso soup, and we got into our pyjamas and settled on the couch to watch this old movie Sophie loves called *The Remains of the Day*. We've watched it tons of times before, and the result is always a floor carpeted with wet tissues, so you wouldn't think it was the best film to make Soph happy again, but she actually likes watching it most when she's down. 'Sometimes you *need* to cry,' she says. 'Sometimes it makes you feel better to let it all out.'

When I'm upset, sometimes I put on 'Hurt' by Johnny Cash. It breaks my heart but, at the same time, it pieces it together. It helps to know I'm not the only person in the universe who's sad.

We were settled on the couch, ready to get good and wallowy, when Soph's phone rang. It was her friend Polly.

'Oh no. Oh, babe. Oh, Polly,' Sophie moaned, her forehead crinkled. It seemed Polly wasn't having a great day, either.

'What? You want me to come over? Well, I'm in my pyjamas. I hadn't planned to—'

Sophie bit her lip. I could hear Polly sobbing on the other end. 'I'll be right there,' Soph sighed finally.

She hung up and turned to me with a grimace. 'Sorry, Clemmie. Polly's just found out Tim cheated on her with a sixteen-year-old at a party last weekend. I don't *want* to go, but she needs me.'

'Go,' I said, waving her away. 'I've got Anthony Hopkins and Emma Thompson to keep me company. You save Polly.'

But after Soph left, I found I wasn't really in the mood for Anthony and Emma and their stiff-upper-lip British melancholy. Something else was calling me.

My purple notebook.

The thoughts in my head.

Words.

I didn't know which words, until I started writing. I was surprised by the ones that came.

I'm going to paste the poem in here, but I don't want you to judge me. I don't want you to read anything into it. I don't want you to think I'm in love with the boy – Fred – because obviously I'm not. I only just met him. I don't know what I think about him yet.

But I did know I wanted to write about him.

Click.
Clack.
The watch opens and shuts
and your eyes,
they watch me,
like I am time and space.
Like I can tell you things,
like I can
give you answers.

Click
clack.
The seconds tick by
but I don't hear them.
All I hear
is your voice saying,
'Clementine,'
and, as the sun moves
in the sky above us,
all I see
is your eyes,
seeing
me.

It's only a silly poem, I know, but after I wrote it I was filled with a strange feeling, one I don't think I've experienced before.

I felt . . . infinite. I felt as if things were about to happen. I didn't know what those things might be, but they made me feel giggly. I closed my eyes and leaned my head on my notebook, and I thought about cogs and wheels, and words, and cider-gum leaves.

It's Friday, Ms H, and I'm slightly stressed.

If you actually read this journal when I hand it in each week, you'll know that today is the day of the Big Triple Date. The one with Sam and Chelsea-Grace and Todd and Clara . . . and me and Brent.

The one I'm not at all sure I want to be part of. The one I *have* to be part of, because my two best friends are so looking forward to it.

We're meeting before the movie, at the noodle place at the beach. Cleo and Chels told me this in the lunch room today, and my grump about the whole date thing put me in an argumentative mood.

'Why the noodle place?' I asked. 'There are so many more interesting places to eat in Burnie. Why don't we go to the Rialto for pasta? Or to Fish Frenzy at the beach? Or to Mecca! They do good pizza, and their live music is awesome. The others might like it there. Fergus . . .' I trailed off.

Fergus used to love Mecca. The last time we were there, Fergus's music teacher, Mr Zappa, was playing in a jazz quartet. Heaps of kids from Burnie High went, including Fergus's charming old friend from primary school, Phil. Ioannis Poulos was there, too. He waved at me across the room, and Fergus ribbed me the whole night about him being my boyfriend. Phil kept saying, 'Oh, Clementine. You're breaking my heart. I always thought we were destined to be together!' I liked Phil heaps, back then. I thought he was hilarious.

We all had ice-cream sundaes and the music was fantastic. Afterwards, Mr Zappa thanked us for coming and ended up sitting with us for a coffee. We stayed there way too late, singing and laughing. It was wonderful.

'Anyway, you like those places, too,' I reminded Cleo. 'You loved the risotto you had at the Rialto, when we went there for my birthday.'

'We were *twelve*, Clemmie!' Cleo groaned. 'And, carbs much? Besides, it's better to do what the boys want.'

I was unable to hold back a snort.

'We want to seem *easy*,' Chelsea-Grace added. Cleo and I exchanged a look and burst out laughing.

Chels's brow was furrowed.

'Sorry, Chels,' Cleo drawled when she'd calmed down enough to speak again. Then her eyes flicked to me and she was suddenly, uncharacteristically tentative.

'Clem, we were thinking, too, that it might be an idea to keep the conversation to topics that Todd, Sam and Brent might be interested in. You're always talking to us about your country music and your books . . .'

It might have been true once, Ms H, but I can't remember the last time I talked about books with Cleo. She used to like historical epics, but I don't even know if she reads anymore.

So I haven't told her about the novel Fred loaned me.

I haven't told her that it's unlike any book I've ever read. That it's set in an alternative version of the nineteenth century, where Queen Victoria the *Second* is in power and Neanderthals still exist, not to mention dodos, and everyone flies around in steam-powered airships, including the vampire prime minister. That it's funny and bizarre and marvellous.

I haven't told her I've been learning more about steampunk. That it's a type of story, in which history is re-imagined and things like technology develop differently, often involving steam power. That there's a whole movement that's grown up around it, where people dress in Victorian clothes just for fun – the way Fred does with his bowler hat and his funny cape. Girls wear corsets and puffy skirts and hobnailed boots, or sometimes boyish clothes instead. They make the books come to life.

It's very peculiar. And also seems quite wonderful. But I definitely haven't told Cleo that.

'We're just not sure they're the sorts of things the boys will want to talk about,' Cleo finished.

'So, no books, okay, hon?' Chels confirmed.

'No books,' I sighed.

Chels beamed. 'Good girl. So, next – what are you going to order? Cleo and I decided we'll each have one of the Noodly Natural salads, only without the noodles. And we don't—'

'For dinner?' I interrupted. 'A salad?'

Cleo rolled her eyes. 'Clem. It's not cool to eat lots in front of boys – and besides, noodles would make you bloated in your new dress. Which reminds me, we should go for a run before dinner.'

'I can't. I'm busy. And besides, I'm not going to lose any weight between now and teatime.' I said it grumpily. Cleo's face flushed.

'You know that's not what Cleo meant, Clem,' Chelsea-Grace said softly. 'She just thought it might get us . . . *geared up*, right Cleo? Don't you feel *amazing* after exercise?'

'Sometimes.' I thought of the Latin dance classes we did in sport a while back. Those were fun, and I'd felt energetic and invigorated afterwards. But running? 'I'm not sure *jogging* is the exercise for me, though. It feels as if I'm on a horizontal hamster-wheel, running and running and not *getting* anywhere, and—'

'Don't be silly,' Cleo said firmly. 'You just haven't done it enough yet to know you like it! And we all have a free last period. We can run then, before you're *busy*.'

'All right, all right,' I sighed. 'Get me to a runnery.'

'Huh?' Chelsea-Grace said. Cleo rolled her eyes.

And so, after class, even though what I'd actually like to do is get home early and sit down with a peppermint tea and read Fred's book, to try to relax before this so-called date takes place, I will instead be running laps around the big hamster-wheel again.

And it will be my punishment, Ms Hiller. Punishment for every time I have not told 3CD that I *don't want* to run. Punishment for all these years of being the Clementine *they* want me to be.

I'm home now. I'm not in class. But I need to talk. I'm nervous, Ms Hiller.

It's the belly-churning, hand-trembling sort of nervousness that even a good book and a peppermint tea can't fix.

I could call Cleo or Chelsea-Grace, but I don't want them to know I'm anxious about the date. And Sophie is at Polly's house.

Mum's home for once, because Dad's at a meeting, but she's buried under piles of law journals and I'm under express instructions not to bother her unless it's to bring her cheese-and-pickle sandwiches.

So I'm telling you.

I feel as if I have wasps in my belly.

It's definitely not butterflies. It's not a fluttery, jittery, light-as-a-feather nervousness. It's a biting, *aching* nervousness.

Even though I don't love or even *fancy* Brent, I know tonight is going to be a big deal.

If – and I very much doubt this – Brent and I get along well and he asks me out, I'll— Well, I don't know what I'll do, Ms Hiller. Because I *don't* like Brent in that way, but I don't want to upset him if he does like *me*. And if I turned him down, Cleo and Chelsea-Grace would be so angry . . .

The other scenario – the more likely one – is that Brent *doesn't* like me and is only doing this because he's nice, meaning the whole thing will be awkward and horrible.

I don't know which possibility scares me more.

All I know is that I'm full of wasps. And all I want is to stay home and hide under the doona until tomorrow.

My Favourite Flower is the Pansy by Clementine Darcy

My favourite flower is the pansy, because there are singing pansies in Disney's *Alice in Wonderland*, my favourite Disney movie, based on one of my favourite books. And because they are used as a love potion in *A Midsummer Night's Dream*, which is my favourite Shakespearean play.

And they look like little monkeys.

And because we had them in our garden growing up, and Soph made them into garlands and wreaths, and pretended we were faerie queens.

She was Ginger, and I was Honeysuckle, and there was more magic in the world than we could ever imagine, and that was just the way we liked it.

I like pansies because . . .

May I talk about Friday now?

I can't write about flowers when all I have is Friday on my mind, and how it was a *complete disaster*.

You knew it would be, didn't you? You could not, however, have possibly imagined the extent of the catastrophe.

After my little meltdown, I went to my room and put on my new black dress.

I heard Sophie get home while I was getting ready. 'Wow, little sis,' she said when I came downstairs. She even put her textbook down, and she stood up to check me out. Soph was wearing beige linen pants and a plaid shirt tied at her waist. She looked like Audrey Hepburn. And you know what? I felt a bit Holly Golightly myself, in my swanky dress, with my hair back in a bun and a slick of mascara on my eyelashes.

Sophie dropped me at the restaurant, with a 'good luck' and a hug.

She felt all bones and angles.

Nobody else was there yet, so I took Fred's book from my handbag.

I was immersed in a really exciting scene, about Queen Victoria battling a giant octopus, when Sam walked in.

I had to admit, he did – objectively speaking – look hot. He was wearing a black pinstriped shirt, expensive-looking jeans and designer sneakers. And Chels was right. He did look older. More mature. He *looked* seventeen.

I suddenly felt childish. And *naive*.

'Hey, Clem,' he said casually, as if he said it all the time. As if we were friends. And then he smiled, and it looked . . . practised. As if he smiled like that often, at girls, and he knew the effect it had. His smile was big and white and dazzling. He looked like a male model: all teeth and shiny hair.

'Whatcha readin'?' he asked and I showed him the book.

'Right,' he said. 'Deep.'

I didn't know how to respond to that.

He looked me up and down. 'I love your dress. You look really pretty.'

'Thanks,' I said uncertainly. 'You look . . . nice, too?'

'You're really different from those other two, aren't you?' He fixed his eyes on mine. It wasn't like when Fred looked in my eyes.

'In, um, what way?' I asked.

'You're just *deeper*,' he said, leaning in close. Too close. 'You're deeper, and that makes you more *beautiful* . . .'

I was just wondering, through my shock, which cheesy boy band he'd stolen that line from when he reached over and *put his hand on my knee.*

And that made me angry.

Who did he think he was, touching me like that, without invitation or permission? He might be hot, he might be popular and older, but I *never said he could touch my leg!*

'Get your—' I began, but before I could add *hand off my leg, you creepy pervert,* the door swung open and there, staring at me in absolute horror, were Brent, Todd, Cleo and . . . Chelsea-Grace.

Chelsea-Grace, in her gorgeous, flower-printed dress. Chelsea-Grace, looking at me as though I had just run over her puppy.

'Clem?' she said quietly. 'What's—'

'Hey, isn't she meant to be with me?' Brent looked furiously at Sam.

'I'm not *with* anybody,' I retorted, suddenly conscious that Sam *still* had his hand on my knee. That boy had serious nerve. I tried to slap it away, but he grabbed my hand before I could. Which looked – revoltingly – even more incriminating.

'That's not what it looks like!' Chels marched towards us, her arms crossed. Sam turned from me and found himself eye-level with Chelsea-Grace's chest. He smirked and raised an eyebrow.

And then he slid his hand a bit further up, to my inner thigh.

'Get OFF me,' I snarled and wrenched myself out of his grip, my heart racing.

'What is *happening*?' gasped Chelsea-Grace. 'It's . . . it's not . . .'

'Chels, nothing happened!' I said. 'We were only talking. And then he—'

'Talking about how good your fat thigh felt?' Chelsea-Grace spat.

She didn't say she was sorry. She didn't say she hadn't intended to be mean. Instead, she added, 'You think it's absolutely fine for my boyfriend to touch your thigh?'

'Chelsea-Grace. Honey.' Sam stood up. 'I hate to break it to you, but you're not my girlfriend. Maybe you had a chance tonight – especially in that dress – but the way you're acting now makes me really glad you're not. Because I can just walk straight out of here without feeling guilty.'

Then Sam turned to me. 'I *like* your fat thighs.' He winked and, still staring straight at me, he said, 'Come on, dudes. Let's get out of here.'

As they were leaving, I heard him say to Brent, 'Don't look at me like that, man. You know you would have done the same thing.'

And then we were alone. 3CD. Cleo with her blonde hair twisted into little coils, and her butterfly top showing off her muscular torso; Chelsea-Grace in her sexy, low-cut dress, her brown hair streaked with copper and scrunched into messy waves; and me, in my Holly Golightly dress, the one I had felt so confident in an hour ago. Now, I felt ugly.

I felt ugly and ashamed.

'I really didn't do anything,' I said. 'He just put his—'

Chelsea-Grace buried her face her hands. They were shaking. 'Clem, no,' she said, her voice cracking. She looked up at me, and her face was streaked with tears. They made silvery snail tracks through her mineral foundation. Her eyes were red. 'I know what I saw. Why would you do that?' Her voice had risen. People were starting to look. A table of Burnie High girls held their chopsticks halfway to their mouths as they gawked at us.

'I promise, Chels,' I said, trying to take her hand. She yanked it away.

'I don't believe you!' she cried. 'I can't believe you. This is . . . this has been happening for a while, hasn't it?'

'What? Me and Sam? No! I never even talked to him before tonight!'

'No!' Chelsea-Grace shook her head. '*This*. Us.' She paused for a moment and looked me straight in the eye. 'The end of 3CD.'

My head was swimming. I tried to say 'no', but no sound would come from my mouth. The other people in the restaurant faded into the background and, for a moment, it felt as though Chelsea-Grace and Cleo and I were standing in a bubble that held only us.

It wasn't a good bubble, though, like the one we'd been in for the past few years. It was a sad bubble.

It was a bubble that was about to break.

'We've seen it coming, Clementine.' Cleo stepped forward and put her arm around Chelsea-Grace's shoulder. 'We're your friends, and of course we noticed when you started going through some traumatic stuff at home. That's gone on for ages now, though, and you're still . . . different.'

'Different?' I felt very small as they looked down on me. 'I'm not—'

'*I don't think running is the right sport for me*,' Cleo mocked. Next to her, Chelsea-Grace had her face in her hands again. '*I don't want to go to the concert with you. I'm just going to spend the whole lunch hour outside somewhere and not even tell you where I'm going*. You *are* different, Clem. You're . . .' Cleo sighed. 'You're not *like us*. You're—'

I knew what she was trying to say. *You're plain and daggy, and we're skinny and cool.*

'Don't,' Chels interrupted, shaking her head. 'Don't, Cleo. Please leave it.' She looked just past my shoulder. 'I don't want to talk to you anymore, Clementine. Cleo, I think we should just go.'

Cleo nodded. 'Yeah.'

And then they went. Just like that.

I watched them walk away, through the door and into the car park, and I thought, again, how right they looked together.

I knew it then.

3CD had shattered.

I turned and looked around the restaurant. The other diners were either staring at me or making a good show of pretending they weren't.

I noticed my face was wet. I was crying.

I was crying for the past two-and-a-bit years; for the best friends I'd ever had; and for a future that was big and dark and scary without them in it.

I wanted to yell, *What are you looking at?* to all the staring people, but I couldn't. I'd lost my voice. I'd lost my dignity, too, but that didn't seem to matter anymore. I knew I should be feeling humiliated. I couldn't bring myself to care.

All I cared about was that tomorrow, I wouldn't be going around to Cleo's house with Chelsea-Grace, and watching stupid movies and talking about the dumb stuff they liked. I might have thought it was boring before, but now it was all I wanted to do.

All I cared about was that on Monday morning, when I arrived at school, there wouldn't be any gossiping next to the lockers before first period, or games of cards at lunchtime. I knew the rest of the girls wouldn't want to be friends with me anymore, either. They were more Chelsea-Grace and Cleo's friends than they were mine.

Of course, I thought, there was a possibility that this wasn't *permanent.*

I might wake up to a text tomorrow from Chelsea-Grace saying she'd forgiven me.

I might arrive at school on Monday and find them both standing next to my locker, waiting to fold me up in a big 3CD group hug.

This might just be a blip. A dip in the continuing line-graph that was our friendship.

But something told me that it wasn't. Something told me this was much bigger than Sam putting his hand on my thigh. There'd been something rotten in the state of 3CD long before that had happened. Knowing this made me feel as if I was falling into a big, deep well with no bottom. As if I was being carried away by the wind.

It made me *terrified.*

I rubbed at the tears on my face. I blew my nose and I ignored the still-staring people. I pulled the elastic from my hair and let it fall limply down. I retrieved the hoodie I'd rolled up and stuffed in my handbag to put on after the movie as a shield against the cold night air.

I wasn't Holly Golightly from *Breakfast at Tiffany's* anymore.

I was Patricia Neal's character, Emily Eustace Failenson. Abandoned by the only real friends I'd ever had. Alone and miserable.

All I could think to do was go to my big brother and ask him – like the last time, in primary school, with Leah Parker – to make it all better again.

At home, I went straight up to Fergus's room and knocked on his door.

Mum was still working. Soph and Dad were still out, but I could see a thin sliver of light coming from underneath Fergus's door. I knocked gently.

'Hello?' I called out. There was no answer, but I heard him shifting inside. 'Hey, Fergus?' I tried.

Still nothing.

I lowered myself to the floor and sat cross-legged, facing his bedroom door.

'Fergus, I know you can hear me,' I said. 'And I know you probably won't answer – but I wanted to tell you that I had a really awful night tonight.

'Before, Fergus, when I had nights like this, I'd talk to you and you'd tell me a joke to make me feel better. You always knew how to make me feel better.

'And I understand that you're mad at me. I *understand* that. I know I *said* something that made you feel . . . I know this is my fault.

'But I lost my two best friends tonight, Gus. Chelsea-Grace and Cleo. We had a fight in the middle of the noodle place, and everyone stared, and it – the fight – it seemed as though it was over nothing but it wasn't, I don't think. They say I've changed, but I know I haven't. I know it's really Chelsea-Grace and Cleo who've changed. But that doesn't matter, in the end, does it? What matters is *we've* changed. 3CD. We're not the same as we were and that's . . .

'I'm scared, Fergus. I've lost my only friends, and I feel as if Sophie doesn't want to be friends with me either anymore, now that she's at university and has all these *grown-up* problems. And you . . .

'Fergus, I want you to know that *I* know it's my fault you're in there. And I want to get you out. I can't lose Chelsea-Grace and Cleo and Sophie *and* you. Especially not you.

'Fergus, you're my big brother and I want you back. If I figure out a way to get you back, will you . . . would you . . .'

There was still no sound coming from Fergus's room. I didn't know if that meant he was listening or ignoring me. I tucked my knees to my chest and leaned my cheek on top of them. My tears soaked through my new patterned tights. I held my hand up to Fergus's door and placed my palm flat against it.

'Fergus, I'm sorry I haven't tried harder,' I said. 'I thought you'd snap out of it, but you're not going to, are you? So it's up to me to help you, isn't it? I don't know how I'm going to do it yet, but I'll figure it out. I know Sophie thinks I'm naive and dreamy, and Dad thinks I'm just someone to do silly dances with, and Mum – well, Mum's so busy I don't even know what she thinks of me; probably that I'm still twelve years old. I can help you, though. I can. I promise I can.'

I got to my feet and stood for a few moments, biting my lip and looking at the door, willing it to swing open; willing my funny, talented, sturdy, determined brother to step out of there, put his arms around me, and hold me in a big bear hug like he used to as he told me everything would be okay.

But I knew that couldn't happen. Because I knew Fergus *didn't* know that anymore.

It's my second day of friendlessness, Ms Hiller.

I sat alone in the lunch room, again, reading a new steampunk book I borrowed from the library. It's very enjoyable. Thrilling and funny. But I haven't laughed once. And I keep reading the same paragraphs over and over again.

I keep coming to the lunch room, hoping that Cleo and Chelsea-Grace and the others will be here, but they've found somewhere new to sit, far away from me. Our old table has been taken over by some Grade 8s. They're always hugging and laughing. They look so joyous.

I wonder if that's how we used to look – 3CD. Before we were broken. Before we split just left of the middle, into two pieces – one Chelsea-Grace-and-Cleo-shaped piece and one Clementine-shaped piece – with a little pile of rubble in the middle that means our jagged edges will never quite fit together again.

I miss them.

We have a history. And they are good people. And I want to fix things with them, somehow. I want to fix Fergus, too. I want everything to go back to the way it was.

Tomorrow, I might not come to the lunch room. I might go somewhere different. It might make the pain less bad.

And I think I might pass my journal in early this week, and ask you to read this entry.

I want someone to listen.

Dear Clementine,

Thank you very much for handing in your journal yesterday. Mrs Wood told me at the beginning of the year that you are an exceptional English student, and indeed, I have been very impressed with how you have applied yourself to this task.

I know you believe you are not learning anything in this class. But perhaps you are, gradually, beginning to discover or create something . . .

I do hope you are able to find a solution to the situation with your friends, and that your brother's issues, in time, resolve.

However, I do not believe that it is your responsibility to 'fix' Fergus. Have you and your family considered that your brother might be suffering from depression? Depression is a mental disorder; like any disease, it requires consultation with a professional and, often, a treatment program. If you are interested, I can direct you to some organisations that may be able to assist you in finding help for Fergus.

Please keep writing, Clementine. I have not given this entry a mark – I do not intend to give any of your writing a mark; so long as you write, you will pass this segment of the course – but I will tell you that you have a charming, engaging voice and a unique turn of phrase. I would very much like to continue reading your work, including your poetry should you choose to include it.

And please do continue to let me know, in future, if there are times when you would particularly like to know that somebody is listening.

Ms Hiller

Dear Ms Hiller,

I know you were only trying to help, but I have to correct what you wrote in your letter.

Fergus doesn't have 'depression'. You don't understand. He's just not that sort of person. Fergus has always been the one to find the funny side of any situation. He's always been the one who laughs things away, and makes everything right again.

Fergus doesn't have depression, Ms Hiller. He's in his room because of me, and because of what happened with Alyssa. And I have a plan for how to make it better . . .

Last night, I typed 'Alyssa Masson' into the Facebook search box.

Thankfully she hadn't made her profile private, so I was able to look at everything, including her wall posts and photos. I was chuffed to see that there were no recent romantic photos, *and* she hadn't deleted the old ones of her and Fergus. Plus, her relationship status was set to single.

And the best thing of all? She had an email address listed in her information. I copied it into a new message and I started to type.

Dear Alyssa,

I don't know if you remember me. I'm Clementine, Fergus's younger sister. I know it's crazycakes – emailing you like this – but I was wondering if you'd mind coming over sometime? Maybe in the next couple of days, if you're not busy? I only want to have a chat. I totally understand if you think it's too weird, but I'd so appreciate it. Anyway, hope to hear from you!

Hugs,

Clem

She hasn't emailed me back yet, Ms Hiller, but it's going to work. You wait and see. It's all part of my grand plan.

On which note, I do wish I had a plan for how to deal with Sam Peterswalds, too . . .

You see, while I've been pursuing Alyssa Masson on Facebook, Sam Peterswalds has been pursuing *me*. And I'm not quite sure what to do about it.

I don't like him. And I know that Chelsea-Grace still *does*.

That's the wonderful thing about Facebook – it allows you to view other people's lives and activities, whether you are still a part of them or not.

It lets you know that your former best friend is still in love with the boy who groped your thigh.

I find Facebook boring. I don't care who had Sultana Bran for breakfast, or whose dog is chewing on their shoe. And I'm certain no one wants to hear that my hair has reached new heights of blah-dom, or that I'm listening to Steve Earle while I eat my lunch. I hardly ever look at my profile, and I never update it. Which is probably why Chels and Cleo have not remembered to un-friend me. So I can still see their statuses and their wall posts.

Last night Chelsea-Grace posted: So, I still love HIM, even though HE won't leave HIS girlfriend. Life sucks.

A new comment soon popped up, from Cleo: Call me, okay?

Then Chenoa Caton commented: Who is he? Wow! This is all very scandalous!

She obviously had no idea that Cleo and Chelsea-Grace were talking about *her boyfriend.*

Chelsea-Grace ignored Chenoa and replied to Cleo's comment: Don't feel up to talking about it, hon. Too sad.

Cleo wrote: Don't be a wuss. I'm coming over with a movie. And you know what? It damn well ain't going to be that *Love and Other Catastrophes*!

Love and Other Catastrophes is my favourite movie, Ms Hiller.

I kind of miss *Love and Other Catastrophes* . . . Chelsea-Grace replied.

Cleo: Babe, no you don't, okay? We're not going there. Right?

Chelsea-Grace: Okay. Thanks, Cleo. See you soon. Don't bring chocolate, though. I'm fat.

Cleo: Okay. We can do crunches while we watch the movie.

After they'd both gone offline, Gemma commented: Do you two ever talk about anything meaningful? Like the war in Syria? Or the global financial crisis? Or climate change? *Sigh* It's all well and good to run away from the real world sometimes, but you need to live in it occasionally.

And then Chenoa replied: I can talk to you about wars and stuff, Gemma. If you want to? Would you like to chat?

But Gemma had already gone.

While all of this was going on, Sam Peterswalds sent me a direct message.

Hey Clem.

I'm sorry our time together on Friday night ended so quickly. That sucked. Brent is really sorry, and he wants you to know there are no hard feelings. He thinks you're hot, but he could see there was chemistry between me and you, so it's all good.

Anyway, Todd tells me you're fighting with Cleo and Chelsea-Grace. Does this mean it might be okay for us to hang out? Let me know.

By the way, I don't feel anything for Chelsea-Grace. She's delusional. And I'm just working out how to dump Chenoa. It's complicated, because she's a bit mental, and I'm worried that if I just drop her she'll key my car or burn my signed Essendon guernsey.

Believe me, Clem, it's you I want. And you won't regret going out with me. We'll have a really good time. I have a car and everything. Think about it.

I didn't reply, of course. But I did spend a short time looking through his photo albums. In every single picture, he wore that smarmy, self-satisfied grin. In most of them, he was flexing his pecs or pulling up his T-shirt to show his sixpack. But I didn't find it at all enticing, Ms Hiller. In fact, it made my *own* stomach turn.

It's definite. Sam is *not* the boy for me.

The Most Interesting Person in Class Today
by Clementine Darcy

I DON'T KNOW IF YOU'VE NOTICED, MS HILLER, BUT THERE'S A NEW BOY IN OUR CLASS TODAY!

Did you set this writing exercise with me in mind?

The most interesting person in class today is . . . Fred. The boy! His actual name is Frederick Paul. And of course you've noticed he's in our class – I know his full name because that's how you introduced him. He's transferred from 9A to 9B because he wants to take history *and* philosophy, and he can only do that if he's in 9B. So now he's here!

And why is he interesting?

Well, he *is* wearing a cape . . .

Also, he hasn't stopped writing since you explained the project to him. And I can see – not that I'm snooping, it's only that he's sitting right in front of me – that he's drawing little diagrams up the margins of the pages. They look like engineering diagrams. Like pictures of machines. He's drawn a person, too – a person wearing a top hat and goggl—

♡

Frederick Paul just turned and smiled at me!

'Hello, Clementine,' he whispered.

'Hi Fred,' I whispered back, and I felt my face going the

same colour as the capsicum on Gemma Gleave's 'Vivacious Vegan' T-shirt.

He turned back to the front, and now I can't stop staring at him. I wonder if he can feel me watching. Probably not. He just keeps drawing – making more and more machines. And other things, too. Rockets and strange metal fish and parasols and muskets and odd musical instruments.

Ms Hiller . . . *who is this boy*?

Alyssa wrote back to me!

I'm so excited, Ms Hiller. It feels as if, finally, things might be taking a turn for the better.

I printed the email for you. She says she'll come over!

Hi Clem,

Of course I remember Miss Clementine Darcy! How lovely to hear from you. And of course, if you need me to come and see you, I will. Are you in trouble? Or is it about Fergus? Never mind. Whatever you need, I'll be there. I've got work during the day, but I can come over one night afterwards. Just let me know when works best for you.

Take care, Clem.

Alyssa

Isn't she lovely, Ms Hiller?

I was expecting her to be hesitant. I thought she'd feel odd about seeing Fergus. But if she didn't want to see him, she would have said something, surely.

I was so thrilled after reading her email that I had to write about it.

You could have turned away
and walked
into the shadows.
You could have said 'no'
and shaken your head
and looked away from us.

You could have forgotten
all that was.
You could have abandoned him
to that room,
to that darkness,
but instead you smiled
and you reached out
and you let us see
there's hope.

I know, Ms Hiller, that what I wrote in the poem isn't strictly true. Alyssa didn't smile and reach out. Not literally, anyway, but it feels as if the email is a reaching-out and a smiling.

It feels as if she's given us something to believe in. Me and Fergus.

I feel for the first time in months like I might get my big brother back.

And that makes everything else feel less painful: when Cleo and Chelsea-Grace walked past me in the corridor earlier and wouldn't meet my eye; when Sam put a note in my locker saying 'You look hot today'; when Sophie yelled at me last night for eating some of her fat-free yoghurt. I didn't get as upset as I usually would about any of those things, because of that email. Because of Alyssa. Because things are about to get better.

And Fred Paul carried my books to class. It was an old-fashioned thing to do, I know, but I guess that makes it a Fred Paul thing to do. And I really liked it.

He's sitting next to me right now, and every so often I sneak a glance at him. Once I caught him glancing back at me.

I know he's probably quite mad and he's definitely strange, but when I close my eyes I can picture us kissing. And the thought of kissing him makes me even happier.

I don't know if I can handle this much happy.

I probably shouldn't trust it too much, Ms Hiller, because it's when you let yourself be really, truly happy that things come crashing down.

The Worst Day of My Life by Clementine Darcy

Today, when we came to class, you had written something on the whiteboard:

'Every step you take is your own, and the direction in which it takes you is the one you choose. Only dead fish swim with the stream.'

You looked at us. 'We are not defined by the moments of our life. We are not defined by our histories. Every second of every day is the second we can change it all.' You perched on the corner of your desk and smoothed your argyle jumper. 'But it helps to look at the moments we have lived and see what effect they had on the person we have become. It helps us to shed those moments. To move forward.'

And then you wrote today's topic on the board. 'The Worst Day of My Life.'

I didn't start writing straight away. I stared at the words *you'd* written first – about the dead fish.

And I thought: *I am swimming with the stream.*

Worse than that, my brother is not swimming at all. He's sunk to the bottom of the fish pond. He's not even floating anymore.

He's dead inside.

The only way to save him is for me to swim like crazy, for the both of us. I have to do it for him, Ms Hiller. I have to fix him.

The worst day of my life was when Fergus went into his room and didn't come back.

The day started normally. Fergus came down to breakfast with us, and he said 'Good morning' and made himself a strong coffee and thumbed through the entertainment section of the paper, like he always did. But then, when Dad put some toast in front of him, he said, 'I'm not hungry.'

'Maybe you'd prefer if I made you a . . . yak brûlée?' I asked in a dodgy French accent. Ever since he'd first started his training, I'd made fun of the posh-sounding menu items he had to create, changing the ingredients to the most bizarre things I could think of. 'A gnu bouillabaisse, perhaps? Meerkat mousse? What do you *sink?*'

I was trying to cheer him up, Ms H, in my own clumsy way. Because I'd discovered something the night before.

After the birthday dinner, in the middle of the night, I woke up thirsty. I got up for a glass of blackcurrant cordial, and I was in the pantry when Fergus came into the kitchen talking on his phone.

'Please, Lyssie. Don't do this to me.'

I shrank back into the darkness.

'But he's my friend,' Fergus said. 'How could you . . . I mean, it's Phil! He's my best . . . I know. I know you told me, but I still thought . . . Come on, Lyssie. It's been a horrible week . . . You heard about work? Of course, Phil told you. It's crap, Lyssie. I did nothing wrong. I just didn't turn up one . . . No. I don't want to talk about *why*. I don't want to talk about it at all.'

There was a long pause then. I held my breath. Finally, he spoke again.

'I understand, Lyssie. I'm not Phil. I'm not *smart*. I'm not studying to be an architect. I'm not even that good a chef. I'm pathetic. I know you have to go, Lyssie. Phil's waiting. Okay. I love you. Lyssie? Lyssie, it's my *birthday* . . . I know. I know you never meant to . . . I know that . . . I just love you. I love you. Lyssie?'

I heard Fergus's phone beep as he hung up. I heard it clatter as he dropped it to the floor. I heard him sit down, heavily, on one of the kitchen stools. And then I heard something I hadn't heard for a very long time.

I heard Fergus cry.

Some time later – long enough that every limb on my body had gone to sleep – I heard the scrape of Fergus's chair against the kitchen tiles, and I heard the creak of the fifth step as he went upstairs.

I pushed myself up unsteadily from the pantry floor. I looked at the bottle of Ribena. I couldn't stomach it anymore. My belly ached with worry. Fergus and Alyssa had broken up. And Fergus had lost his job?

Why hadn't he told us?

The next morning, though, Fergus seemed normal. Quieter than usual, perhaps, but not crying. Not calling himself *pathetic*. And so I thought everything was all right, and cracked my dumb meerkat mousse joke.

'Do you not find me *funnee*, *Monsieur Losér*?' I followed on, making fun of him, the way we always made fun of each other. I poked him on the arm. 'Remember what Jimmy Buffett says, hey? We'll go insane if we can't laugh!'

Fergus looked, slowly, up from his plate. His eyes were empty. 'Sorry,' he said. And then he went upstairs. To his room. And closed the door.

'Oh no,' I groaned.

'What's up, honey?' Dad asked.

'He lost his job,' I said, quietly. 'But he seemed fine this morning, and so I thought . . . I shouldn't have teased him like that.'

Dad looked shocked. 'He lost his job?'

'And Lyssie dumped him,' I added, wincing.

Dad sat down on the kitchen stool. 'Oh no,' he said quietly. 'Poor Gus.'

'I'm going to talk to him.' I pushed my stool back roughly and sprinted up the stairs, two at a time.

I knocked on Fergus's door. 'Come on, Fergus,' I said. 'I'm sorry about what I said. I'm sorry I made you angry. I know you mucked up at work. And with Alyssa. Do you want to talk?'

For ages, there was silence. Then Fergus said, 'Piss off, Clementine.'

I tramped slowly back down the stairs. Hot tears rolled down my cheeks.

I stayed home from school that day. I told Dad I felt sick, and he didn't question me. He and Mum stayed home, too (a big deal for Mum), and had hushed conversations in their bedroom, with the door locked. I mostly stayed in my room. A few times, though, I went up to Fergus's door and knocked, softly.

He didn't answer.

'Do you think he's okay?' I asked Mum tearfully when she and Dad came to visit me.

Mum put her arms around me and squeezed. She kissed the top of my head and said, into my hair, 'I don't know.'

One year on, we still don't know, Ms Heller.

One year on, Fergus still won't come out of his room, at least not when we're around. We know he emerges while we're at work and school. Food is disappearing. Books get taken from the bookshelves and put back. He borrowed my *Doctor Who* series once.

He's alive. But he's drifting. He's floating away.

I mucked everything up. I have to make it right again.

I don't feel like writing real stuff today, Ms H.

So here is a poem I wrote:

You came
and I thought:
Now things will be better.
You're here and he
will see you and he'll
smile
and everything
will be normal again.
You hugged me and
we sat
together
at the kitchen table.
Talked.
We talked about work
and school
and all those things that
seem unimportant
when compared with
what I really wanted to talk about.
And then,
as we talked,
you said that name.
'Phillip.'

And the way you said it,
it was like you had a flower petal
in your mouth,
and your cheeks turned pink
and my heart shrivelled.
And then they came.
My mother and father.
And I thought they'd be pleased
to see you, too,
but they made me come
to another room
and they told me I'd done wrong.
And I heard,
from above me,
the sound of someone on the landing.
A heavy sound.
'Is she here?' he said.
And I called back, 'Yes,'
and he told me
he'd never forgive me.

I tried to talk to Chelsea-Grace today.

I didn't plan it. If I had, I definitely wouldn't have chosen today to do it. I would have picked a time when I felt positive and confident.

Today I felt weighted. Heavy. So full of dark things.

I didn't sleep the other night, after Alyssa came over. After Fergus said he'd never forgive me. After Mum and Dad told me I'd messed up, big time, and that I should have left well enough alone.

They looked so angry, Ms Hiller.

And then Sophie came home, and Mum and Dad told her what had happened, and she was angry too. She said I was a silly little girl.

I went to my room and I cried and, for a while, I thought about giving up, but then I remembered what you'd said. About the dead fish.

I still want to fix Fergus, Ms Hiller. I *can't* believe that was my only chance and I ruined it. I have to hope there's another way.

I spent the past two nights thinking about how I could make things right. By the time this morning came, I still had no answer, and I had a head full of sludge and a heart full of stones.

So it wasn't the best time to talk to Chelsea-Grace. Sometimes the stream takes you in directions you're not ready for. But I guess it's still up to you what you do when you arrive.

I was at my locker, looking for my notebook, when I heard her voice. 'So I'll see you after school, okay? All right. Bye bye, hon!'

It was at that moment that my hardcover copy of *Ulysses* decided to make a leap for freedom from the depths of my locker. 'Oh, holy freaking doughnuts,' I cursed as it connected with my forehead.

'Clem, are you okay?' Chels stopped in front of me. 'Oh, eek!' She touched her fingers to my forehead and held them up before my face. They were red and wet. 'That must really hurt.'

'It's . . . a big book.' I felt slightly woozy.

What I did next should make you proud, Ms Hiller. This is the part where I was brave.

Or perhaps concussed.

'I'm really sorry, Chels,' I said quickly. 'I never meant to hurt you, with Sam. I didn't encourage him at all. I don't like him at all.'

Chelsea-Grace looked at her feet. Her face had gone scarlet.

'I promise,' I said gently. I reached out and put my hand on her arm. And she didn't flinch away. She let me leave it there.

'What's going on?' I'd been so fixated on Chelsea-Grace I hadn't noticed Cleo approach. She stood beside Chels, her hands on her hips. Her eyes flicked to my forehead, but then they narrowed.

'Well, I was just telling Chelsea-Grace—'

'Clem, stop!' she cried, and the anger in her eyes was real. She wasn't enjoying this drama. Cleo was really furious with me. 'Please stop. Don't hurt her even more.' She took Chelsea-Grace's arm. 'You've already done enough. Come on, Chels.'

'I . . . I have to go,' Chelsea-Grace whispered. There were tears in her eyes. As she walked away, Cleo extended an arm and Chelsea-Grace sank into it, leaning her head on Cleo's shoulder.

And I thought my heart would break.

'They're your friends?'

I turned to see Fred Paul standing behind me, in knickerbockers, holding a unicycle. I sighed. 'Not anymore, I don't think.'

Fred nodded. 'May I accompany you to class?' he said.

As we walked, I pulled the book he'd loaned me from my satchel. 'Sorry,' I said.

'Whatever for?'

'Well, both for taking so long to return it to you, and for the Worcestershire sauce stain on page 134.'

'Did you like it?' he asked.

'It made me want to live in Victorian England. I wanted to go back in time.'

'You can, you know.' Fred's hazel eyes sparkled.

I looked at him curiously. 'What do you—' A drop of blood dripped onto my arm, and my hand flew to my forehead. I'd forgotten all about my injury-by-flying-Great-Work-of-Literature.

Fred reached into his pocket and pulled out a crisp white handkerchief. Gently, he dabbed at the cut. When he was done, his perfect handkerchief was tainted with scarlet splodges.

'I'm so sorry,' I said.

'Never mind,' he said softly. 'Are you all right?'

I nodded. 'Better now.'

At that moment, Sam, Brent and Todd walked out of a classroom into the corridor. Sam spotted me, said, 'Go on, guys. I'll catch you up,' and headed my way.

'Shall I leave you alone?' Fred asked.

'No,' I said quickly. The last thing I wanted was to be alone with Sam Peterswalds.

Sam leaned on the wall, blocking my way forward. 'Well, if

it isn't my lucky day,' he said.

'Hello, Sam,' I said, as politely as I could manage. 'I'm just going into class.'

'Can we talk later?' Sam stepped closer, sliding across the wall like a copperhead snake. He looked down at me, the corners of his lips curling up. Now he wasn't a snake – now he was the Cheshire cat. And he stared at me as if I was a saucer of cream. He didn't even seem to notice the blood.

'I'd better get in now, anyway.' Fred indicated our classroom door.

'Me too,' I said quickly. 'Sorry, Sam.'

I wasn't really, though.

Sam shrugged. 'Another time, Clem. I'll keep trying.'

'He seems a bit of a nasty fellow,' Fred said – observantly – as Sam walked away.

'He is,' I agreed.

'And he likes you?'

'I'm not sure *like* is the correct word.' I sighed.

'He covets you,' Fred said, nodding. 'And you don't want to be coveted.'

'Not by him,' I said firmly.

Then something wonderful happened, Ms Hiller, I'll give you that. One wonderful thing in the midst of this heavy, dark day. Fred reached out and took my hand. 'Then I'll just have to protect you,' he said.

I'm sorry, I know I'm meant to be writing about happy memories.

But I can't think of anything happy today. I'm all filled up with sad.

Last night was another bad night at our house, Ms Hiller.

My parents had finally *almost* forgiven me for inviting Alyssa over. They'd realised I was only trying to help. They knew I hadn't intended to make things worse.

How was I to know that seeing Alyssa would make Fergus angry? Or that Alyssa would cry and say she thought it was better for everyone if she just put Fergus behind her?

That was what upset me most of all, Ms Hiller: that someone could want to put my brother behind them. That someone could want to forget him.

But I forgive her, Mr Hiller, because she also said she loved Fergus. She said she never wanted to leave him. She just couldn't handle his sadness. She wanted to be happy. Phil makes her happy. You can't be mad at someone for wanting to be happy.

And even though it didn't play out in exactly the way I'd planned, Alyssa's visit (while undeniably a horrible disaster) changed something in our house.

For so long now, my parents have been saying that Fergus will get over this in his own time. That he's an adult. That we can't *make* him do anything. But it's been a year. A year of Dad going to Centrelink on Fergus's behalf; a year of Mum and Dad paying his car and phone registrations, even though he never uses his car or his phone; a year of waiting. After what happened with Alyssa, Dad decided, finally, that he had to do something.

At six-thirty last night, Elizabeth arrived.

She was wearing a bright-red shirt, black skirt, awesome black patterned tights and red knee-high boots. Her hair was longer at the front than it was at the back. It was dyed bluish-black and shot through with chunks of burgundy. She didn't look like a caseworker. She looked like an indie filmmaker.

Mum had made a special effort to be there. She showed Elizabeth into the front room, where I was pretending to do my homework.

'Elizabeth, this is our daughter Clementine. We have another daughter, Sophie. She's at a lecture this evening.'

'Clementine. What a lovely name,' said Elizabeth. 'I always wished I had an unusual name. Elizabeth is so dull. And my middle name is Jane. Elizabeth Jane Smith. Yuck.'

'My middle names are Alwyn and Shirley,' I said, 'after my grandma and my favourite auntie.'

'Lucky you. All great names! I think Jane was my dad's cocker spaniel!'

She smiled then, and I smiled back. I felt as though I could trust Elizabeth. I hoped Fergus would feel the same way.

'Can I stay?' I asked Mum.

'Of course,' she said. 'This affects our whole family.'

'So how will this work?' Dad asked Elizabeth.

'I guess that depends on Fergus,' she said. 'What I would like is for one of you to go up to his room and ask him to come down and see me.'

'You can't make him come?' I asked.

Elizabeth shook her head. 'Sorry, Clementine. I can't. He has to decide that for himself.'

'He won't come down,' I said, my chin trembling. 'And it's my fault.'

'Clemmie.' Mum stroked my hair. 'You know that's not true.'

'You said it was!' I cried, pulling away. 'You said I mucked everything up, by inviting Alyssa here.'

Mum sighed. 'I'm sorry for getting angry at you, Clem. I shouldn't have. But now isn't the time to discuss that. Not in front of Elizabeth.'

'It's fine,' said Elizabeth gently. 'When this sort of thing happens, it's hard on everyone. There may be a time when you decide you want family counselling, to work through the impact this has had on all of you. But for now, it would be wonderful if we could ask Fergus to come down and have a chat.'

'We can try,' said Dad, 'but as I told you on the phone, he very rarely leaves his room. I think it's the only place he feels safe.'

'I'm hoping he will come to feel safe with me,' said Elizabeth. 'But it might not happen quickly. This might be a long journey. We might make the first step tonight. We might not. If it is indeed depression that we're looking at, it's a tricky beast. It takes time to tame it.'

'Depression?' I said, feeling so quiet and small. 'So it *is* . . .'

Elizabeth nodded. 'It might well be, Clem. From what your dad has told me. But I'll need to talk to Fergus to be sure.'

'But *depression*—' I felt hollow inside, even saying the word.

'Is maybe not what you think it is, Clem,' Elizabeth said. 'It's an illness, like cancer, or diabetes. It's not just somebody feeling a bit blue. And it's not something a person can simply snap out of.'

'It's not something that can be fixed?' Now I really was going to cry. Everything I'd thought and believed was wrong.

Elizabeth smiled and took my hand. 'Of course it can be fixed. And I'm the best person to implement that. But Fergus needs to work with me. He needs to want to change things.'

'I'm going to get him.' I jumped up.

'Clem—' Mum called after me, but it was too late – I was already leaping up the stairs.

'Fergus!' I banged on his door. 'There's a woman here to see you. Her name's Elizabeth. Will you come down, please?'

I waited. Silence leaked from Fergus's room. I tried again.

'Gus? Come on. She's come all this way to see you. You can't let her down.

'Fergus?

'Fergus Stephen Douglas Darcy, come on! I'll break your door down!

'Fergus, seriously, this is so not cool.

'Fergus!!!'

Finally, I heard Fergus's bed creak. I imagined his feet padding over the carpet. I pictured his hand resting on the door. And then . . .

'Make her go away.' His voice was so close. It made my heart hurt. A moment later, I heard the creak again as he returned to his bed.

I walked glumly down the stairs. 'He won't come,' I told them.

'Don't feel bad about it, Clementine,' said Elizabeth. 'We can't always make other people do what we want them to. As I said, Fergus has to do this himself.'

'But that's what everybody's been saying, and nothing's happening!' I protested. 'At least I tried! If you just wait for him, nothing *will* happen. You said you can fix him, but you don't know my brother.'

And I meant it – because the one thing that hasn't changed

about Fergus this past year is his *stubbornness*. Fergus has never liked being told what to do. He's always done things his own way.

At the start of Grade 10, Fergus told Mum and Dad he wasn't going back to school. He said the teachers wanted to fill his head up with stuff he didn't want to know.

'I like learning,' he said. 'But I want to learn what *I* want to learn. The teachers at school teach the same thing every year. You can tell by the way they drone on that they've said it a million times. Their brain isn't even thinking about it anymore; their mouths are just moving. Their eyes are dead. Their minds are dead, and they're trying to make us have dead minds, too. I want to learn cooking. I'm going to go around to all the restaurants and get a job as an apprentice. That's my decision, and it's final.'

Mum and Dad tried everything to get him back to school. They tried grounding him. They tried cutting off his allowance and taking away his Xbox. Nothing worked. Gus was a racehorse with his blinkers on.

It was only after he'd gone around to every restaurant and cafe in Burnie, Wynyard, Penguin and Ulverstone and been told by every chef that he needed to finish Grade 10 to be taken on as an apprentice that he relented. For the next year, Fergus did the bare minimum in all classes except for cooking and music, and the minute he finished Grade 10, he was out of there and working in a restaurant.

Fergus was stubborn then. He is even more stubborn now. Because something very important has changed.

Fergus wasn't afraid, back then. At least, I didn't think he was. I thought nothing frightened him. But now he's definitely scared. I know it. And he doesn't know how to deal with it. So he isn't.

'He needs to be given a big shove,' I said. 'Or else he'll never come out.'

'No, Clementine,' Dad said. 'You tried the big shove, with Alyssa. And that ended—'

'Badly, I know. I *understand* that. I understand now that I can't fix Fergus. Elizabeth *is* the best person to do it, but I think—'

'I'm sorry, Clementine, but I'm afraid a big shove might be counterproductive,' Elizabeth said. 'How do you think Fergus will react if we try to wrench him away by force from the place he feels safe? This is likely to be a gradual process. So you need to focus on getting on with your own life. Try to take your mind off it. Try to think, right now, of something you'd really like to do. Somewhere you'd like to go. Someone you'd like to see . . .'

Elizabeth smiled at me, and winked.

And I thought of Fred Paul.

Fred and I were sitting underneath the cider gum.

It was lunchtime. I was eating a cheese and salad sandwich, on soy-and-linseed bread. Fred was eating cucumber sandwiches from his wicker picnic basket. He had a teapot of Earl Grey brewing. I was trying to think of a way to politely ask for a cup. It smelled so good.

I was still staring at the teapot when Fred took my hand. 'Clementine, I was wondering if I might ask you . . .' He trailed off and looked down at my fingers, intertwined in his. 'I'm sorry, Clementine. I should have asked your permission before I did that.'

My heart flapped its wings and took flight.

'It's fine,' I said softly. 'It's nice.' I knew I was blushing. I didn't care.

Fred smiled. His dimples made little indents in his cheeks and I wanted to stick my finger into one of them.

Is that peculiar?

I cleared my throat to cover my embarrassment. 'So, what were you going to ask me?'

Fred's forehead creased. He looked very serious all of a sudden. 'Well, I *was* going to ask you to accompany me . . . somewhere. But I think I may have changed my mind.'

My heart sank. 'Well, okay. I mean, that's all right. Don't feel you have to—'

'Oh, it's not that! Not at all! I certainly wish to ask you. But, Clementine, I have to warn you, this place, it's . . . Well, some people – your friends – might think . . . What I'm trying to say is that you might not think it's very cool.'

I stared at Fred. What was he on about? 'Fred, *I'm* not cool. My friends are, but I'm not. And I don't want to be. I want to be a flying fish!'

Fred laughed. 'I love it,' he said. 'So, Miss Fish, shall I tell you about the BSS?'

'BSS?'

'Burnie Steampunk Society.'

'Burnie . . . what now?'

'Burnie Steam . . . You read the book I gave you, right?'

I nodded. 'Yes. And I know now there's a steampunk *movement* . . .' I noticed the impressed look on Fred's face and felt self-conscious. 'Um, but there's seriously a society for it? *Here?* In *Burnie*?'

Fred nodded. 'Indeed!'

'Well . . . jeepers!' Now *I* was impressed. I know Burnie is changing. I know there's all sorts of stuff that wasn't here in my parents' day, like the Makers' Workshop, and the big creepy octopus thing down at the beach, but a Steampunk society, here in Burnie?

Surprising. And *intriguing.*

'So what do you do, exactly? In your steampunk society?' I asked.

'Well, fundamentally,' Fred said, 'we are a conglomerate of people who really appreciate steampunk fiction, and the Victorian era aesthetic, and we come together on a weekly basis to talk about what novel we're reading, or any interesting developments in steampunk generally. Then, every month, we hold a Victoriana ball, where we dress up in Victorian clothes and eat Victorian-era foods, and play cricket and croquet. It would be wonderful if you'd join us.'

Suddenly, all I could think of was Cleo and Chelsea-Grace, and how their faces would look if they saw me. Playing croquet.

In a bonnet.

Fred inclined his head, examining my face. 'You're worried about what people will think.'

I nodded silently, and felt terrible. I'd just told Fred I wanted to be a flying fish. I wasn't flying. I wasn't even swimming.

'Everyone worries, at first. But in time, it ceases to matter, the opinions of others. In time you get lost in it all. And the people who go to the balls? Clementine, they don't *care*. You can dress how you want to, and be exactly yourself. It's one of the wonders of it. And, if it helps, there are several members from Burnie High. Gemma Gleave is one of them.'

'Gemma Gleave? Really? But she's so busy with all her causes. And she's addicted to her phone! I wouldn't have thought—'

Fred laughed. 'Yes, she is certainly devoted to that thing. Did you notice it has a steampunk case? With a horse in goggles and a helmet riding a unicycle. We bought it for her, for her birthday. And we assist her with her campaigns. That's what BSS is like. We help each other. So . . . will you come?'

I wanted to say yes. But I wavered. It wasn't quite coming to school dressed as a pademelon, but I knew Cleo and Chelsea-Grace would think going to a Victoriana ball was unacceptably weird. That shouldn't have mattered, but it did.

What would you have done, Ms H?

Scratch that. I know what you'd do. You'd go.

I, on the other hand, was about to allow the stream to carry me away. I opened my mouth to say, *I'd love to but I am, tragically, allergic to bustles . . .*

That's when I saw them. Chelsea-Grace and Cleo. Walking by on the oval, arm-in-arm and giggling: a happy, totally-right-together, Clem-less *2CD*. And I grew some fins.

'Maybe I could meet some of the others?' I said. 'And then decide if I want to go to a meeting?'

'Of course.' Fred's grin was huge and contagious, and I found myself grinning back. 'That sounds like a perfect plan. Now, would you like a cup of tea?'

'I thought you'd never ask.'

'Don't forget to position your pinkie.' Fred held his out at a right angle. I copied, giggling.

'So . . . did you have a Steampunk society back in Sydney?' I asked as I waited for the tea to cool enough to drink.

Fred shook his head. 'No. I didn't get involved in any of this until I moved here.' He shrugged and looked away. His eyes got a sheen to them then, and I knew that wherever his mind was, it wasn't there with me, under the gum tree.

I could hear cogs whirring.

'Why did you move?' I asked, trying to drag his attention back to me. 'Why come to Tasmania from Sydney? Most people go in the opposite direction!'

'Yes.' Fred stared into his tea. 'There was some . . . stuff. Mum thought it might be better if we moved away, and my grandmother lives down here, in Penguin, so it seemed a good enough choice.'

'Stuff?' I asked. 'What sort of stuff?'

'Nothing important.' One corner of Fred's mouth tilted upwards into a sweet half-smile. 'Not now.'

It was clear there was more to the 'stuff' that had happened in Sydney than Fred was letting on, but I remembered what Elizabeth had said, about letting things happen in their own time.

He winked at me then, and it was so adorable I thought I might faint.

'I really thought you'd say no, you know,' he said. 'I didn't pick you as . . . uh . . .'

'A geek?' I smiled broadly.

'Well, yes,' he said. 'Personally, I own it. Being a geek. I take power from the haters and transfer it to myself.'

'Well, all right then!' I sipped my tea. It was delicious. I held the cup up towards my face, so the steam could warm my cheeks. 'Though, what *is* a geek, really? I've always liked Shakespeare and country music and art and poetry – stuff nobody else our age seems to be into – so if that makes me a geek—'

'It makes you *you.*' Fred smiled. 'If you want to call that *geek*, then so be it.'

'I don't really know what I am,' I admitted. 'I used to think I did, but now I'm not friends with Chels and Cleo anymore, I feel . . . lost, I suppose. As though what I thought I was is actually what *they* are. What we were. Not what I am. I think I'm just finding out what I am.'

'Yes, that can take some time.' Fred looked pensive for a moment and shook his head. 'I think it's important to know what you are,' he said finally. 'I think much of the . . . bad stuff happens when you don't.'

'But you know yourself.' I gestured at his clothing. 'Obviously. You know who you are.'

I expected Fred to smile at that, but he didn't. Instead he said, 'Maybe,' and then we lapsed into silence.

Finally, Fred spoke again. 'I think that's what Ms Hiller is trying to do with this writing exercise. I think she's trying to say, *It's all well and good to read what other people think about stuff, but it's more important to work it out ourselves.*'

Is that what you're doing, Ms Hiller? Are you trying to help us to know ourselves?

I wonder if it will work.

A Happy Moment
by Clementine Darcy

Tea.
A poem
about
a happy
moment
drinking tea
beneath
the cider gum
from
china cups
with a boy in crazy clothes,
hot steam
warming
wintered cheeks,
new possibilities
spread
thick
on scones, with cream.
Who knew
life
could take such
funny turns?

Last night I went out with the Burnie Steampunk Society.

Or some of them, at least. The ones Fred thought I should meet before deciding whether to join.

Gemma Gleave was there, and there were two other kids I recognised from school. Their names are Liam Wu and Joshua Phillips, and they're in Grade 10. Then there was Ang Jones, Lucy de Blau and Noel Campisi. They all go to Devonport High. We met up for dinner at Fish Frenzy.

'You'll like them,' Fred had said to me earlier that day, at lunchtime, as we sat again beneath the gum tree sharing tea. 'And it's a good way for me to introduce them to you. It's not a proper meeting. We're simply *touching base* before the ball at the weekend. There's no pressure. They'll love you. Lucy and Ang might even have something you can wear, if . . .'

'If?' I prodded.

Fred's face was reddening. 'Well, as I said, there's the ball on Saturday, so I thought, if you get on with the others . . . They're very nice. Angharad talks a lot, but—'

'*Angharad?*'

Fred nodded. 'Ang, yes – that's her full name. She's lovely, if verbose. And she is quite excited to meet you. As I said, she's even picked some Victorian clothes out for you, just in case.'

'Um, will her clothes fit me?' I asked a little awkwardly. 'I know I'm a bit bigger than—'

'You're perfect, Clementine,' Fred interrupted. 'You're beautiful.'

There was a big pause. Fred looked down at his shiny black dress shoes and bright-white button-up spats.

I didn't know what to say. Fred thought I was beautiful?

I know I shouldn't care, Ms Hiller. I know, as an intelligent, independent, liberated woman of whatever this decade is called, I shouldn't place any store at all in what some boy thinks of my outward appearance.

But Fred isn't just any boy.

And I think he's beautiful, too.

Geeky? Yes.

Slightly bonkers? Absolutely.

But also beautiful.

He's the first boy about whom I can ever imagine the things Chelsea-Grace and Cleo always talked about. The *sex* things.

Not now, Ms Hiller! Not any time soon – but for the first time, I can actually imagine wanting to do it.

Sometime. When the time is right.

'Anyhow,' Fred said at last, still staring at his spats, 'I would estimate that Lucy and Ang are both about your size.' He looked back at me, his cheeks blazing. 'It's a good size,' he said softly.

And he was right, Ms H! Lucy and Ang *are* 'about my size'.

It's not like I've never met anyone my size before – there are plenty of people my size; in fact, my size is the most common size for Australian women. But I've never *hung out* with people my size before. I'm used to being the biggest person in any given group. I'm used to being the fat one.

Don't get me wrong, Lucy and Ang aren't fat. In fact, Ang is one of the most gorgeous people I have ever seen. She's blonde and curvy, with enormous blue eyes and lips you could use as a pillow. She is also *very* tall – a ruler-length at least taller than I am. She has a dusting of freckles on her nose, like cocoa powder, and skin like a porcelain doll. She dresses as if she's in a 1950s movie. At Fish Frenzy, she was wearing a polka-dotted dress and a tight red cardigan. And Fred was right – she talks a lot.

Lucy is *elfin*, and quiet. She has dark cropped hair, olive skin and Cabbage Patch Kid dimples. She wears square, black thick-rimmed glasses, the kind Woody Allen might wear. On her they look feminine and sweet – and yet she's a tomboy. Last night she wore old baggy jeans and a short-sleeved penguin shirt over a long-sleeved stripy one.

Liam, one of the Burnie High guys, is a pierced punk rocker in a leather jacket and ripped jeans. His black hair has chunks of white splashed through it. He looks like a Chinese Joey Ramone.

Joshua, the other guy I'd seen around Burnie High before, looks as though his idea of rock'n'roll is Simon and Garfunkle. He had on brown corduroy trousers and a plaid shirt, buttoned to the neck, and his hair was in a mad red afro.

Liam and Joshua couldn't be more different but, bizarrely, they seem perfect for each other. It only took me a second to realise they were together. And very much in love.

And then there's Noel, Ang and Lucy's mate from Devonport High. Noel is, I suppose, your classic geek. He was wearing a Star Wars T-shirt and a Casio calculator watch. He has a lovely, friendly face, and I figured he must be very nice, being friends with Fred and all, but I couldn't tell for certain because, after saying a smiling 'hello', Noel became . . . preoccupied.

Noel had a new iPhone. Noel liked his new iPhone very much. Noel liked his iPhone so much that it sometimes felt as if Noel and his iPhone were having their own little date at their end of the table, while the rest of us talked steampunk.

'Don't mind him,' Ang said. 'He'd be hopeless if he was actually in Victorian times. Unless he somehow worked out a way to invent a steam-powered iPhone – and if anyone could do that, Noel could. He's a total science freak. That's why he's so into steampunk. Which leads me to my next question.'

Ang finally paused for breath. She narrowed her eyes at me.

'I have to ask: you totally don't look like a typical steampunker, so why do you want to join? Is it because you saw *The League of Extraordinary Gentlemen*? Granted you seem to know a lot about this stuff, so I'm thinking you're not simply another LEG tragic, but if you are, you should just out yourself now. And you know I'm not talking about the graphic novel, right? I mean, Alan Moore is pretty awesome. But the movie's kind of terrible. Apart from the clothes. And Peta Wilson is the bomb. Except her figure would actually have been really unrealistic in those times. She's way too buff. Women didn't exactly go around lifting weights back then, did they, Fred? We played croquet, and the men played cricket. Can you play croquet? Or petanque? If not, you need to learn. But my whole point is, so many people watch that movie and think that's what BSS is all about, but it's not. You know? So if that's why you're joining—'

If Fred hadn't interrupted Ang there, she might have talked her way into the *next* century.

'Clem hasn't decided if she does want to join yet,' Fred said.

'Actually, I have,' I blurted. I hadn't been certain of it until the moment I'd said it, but I *did* want to join the steampunk society. I liked these people. They laughed loudly, and they didn't look around all the time to check if other people were watching them. They were utterly unselfconscious. And they made me feel as if whatever I said, however I acted, that was just fine. Also, there was Fred.

I know I must sound like a broken record, Ms H, but right now I just want to be where Fred is.

He beamed, and I felt even better about my decision. 'Noel, Clem actually got into steampunk because of that book I loaned you.'

Noel looked up. 'Yay.' He went back to his gadget, jabbing at the screen with his thumbs as if he was trying to perform CPR on a mouse.

'I've been reading some other stuff, too,' I added. 'China Miéville and Gail Carriger and Scott Westerfeld, and this other fantastic one about dragons and demons and this family who—'

'All right, all right, we get it! You know your stuff!' Ang held her hands up in the air.

'You've been busy!' said Fred. He looked a bit proud.

'Yes. Well, I've had some time on my hands,' I said, thinking about how many extra hours in the day there seemed to be now I wasn't having sleepovers at Cleo's house or going on Runs of Doom.

'In between writing all your poetry. And passing the time with me under the cider gum.'

'You write poetry?' said Ang. 'That's so Victorian! Have you read these poems, Fred?'

'Not yet.' Fred smiled at me. 'But I hope to soon.'

I felt my cheeks colouring. You know how I feel about showing anyone my poems . . .

'A poetess!' Ang squeezed my hand. '*That is so awesome!* You are going to love BSS!'

'You will love it, Clem,' said Liam, twiddling with one of the many neon badges on his black leather satchel. 'I didn't think it would exactly be my scene, but it turns out steampunk *is* pretty punk. It's naughty and anarchic, and the clothes are totally what Joe Strummer would have worn if he was around in the nineteenth century. It's wicked, isn't it, Josh?'

Joshua nodded. 'Yeah, it's pretty . . . wicked.' He smiled at Liam, shyly, and coughed. 'I never would have said *wicked* before I met this guy.'

Opposites really do attract, I thought.

Just then, Gemma (who'd been tapping away at her phone ever since we got to the restaurant) squealed, '*Noel!*'

'What are you two up to now?' said Fred, raising an eyebrow.

Gemma went bright pink. 'Seriously, Campisi,' she said to Noel. 'Do *not* show him.'

'Relax, Gem.' Noel finally looked up from his phone. He and Gemma locked eyes, *flirtatiously*.

'You two are together?' I said.

'Ever since he offered to hold my parasol for me while I texted.' Gemma sent a coy grin in Noel's direction.

'I had her at *salutations*,' added Noel, his eyes glued to his phone again.

'Everybody hooks up at the balls.' Ang winked.

'No, that's mostly just you,' said Lucy, which gave me a little start because she hadn't said a word for ages.

'Oh, as if you don't have your fair share of admirers,' Ang shot back. 'I *know* you pashed Edward Chamberlain at the last ball.'

'You mean *Axl*,' said Lucy, rolling her eyes. 'Yeah, I did. But from what you told me about Sir Charles Binglefield, it sounds like he was a much better kisser.'

'Hang on, why did you say *You mean Axl*?' I asked. 'Didn't you say his name was Edward?'

'Oh, didn't Fred tell you?' said Ang. 'You have to have a Victorian name. We call them our *nom de vapeur* – *vapeur* means 'steam' in French. My *nom de vapeur* is Scarlett Gadsbloom.'

'Mine is Sir Keith Rollingstone,' said Liam, smirking.

'I told him he would regret that choice once he actually started taking steampunk seriously,' said Joshua, flicking his afro. 'He thinks it's all a big joke right now.'

He and Liam shared a mock-angry look.

'So says the Earl of Cheddar,' said Liam.

'It's a *place*!' Joshua protested.

'It's something you eat on *crackers*!' Liam cried, laughing.

'I'm Gwendolyn Goldsworthy,' said Gemma. 'I wanted to keep my initials. And don't you dare tell her your nickname for me.' Gemma glared at Noel. Noel raised one eyebrow and kept tapping.

My phone beeped. I picked it up. Would you like to accept a new message from FitzwilliamG?

'Is that you?' I asked Noel. Noel's nod was almost imperceptible.

'What? No! *Noel!*' cried Gemma as I clicked on the message.

'Giddy?' I asked, looking up.

'As in *giddy-up*,' Noel explained.

I was none the wiser. 'I still don't—' And then I twigged. 'Ah.'

'That's me,' Gemma groaned. 'GG. Despite the fact that I'm totally against horseracing. It's barbaric. But, to change the subject – please – what will your name be?'

'First thing that comes into your head.' Ang gripped my arm. 'And no. You can't keep the surname Darcy. We have banned the name Darcy, because everybody wanted it, because they're all in love with Colin Firth, even though *Pride and Prejudice* is actually set in Georgian times, not Victorian, and so it's completely—'

'Angharad, let her ruminate,' Fred scolded gently.

'Whatever your lordship wishes.' Ang rolled her eyes and grinned.

'First thing?' Everybody nodded. Noel unglued his eyes from his phone to look at me expectantly.

'Clear out your mind,' said Fred. 'Focus.'

I looked at him helplessly. How could I empty my head? There were too many people inside it, jostling for space. Fergus, Sam, Cleo, Chelsea-Grace. And Fred himself. He was taking up a lot of room.

'Close your eyes,' said Fred. 'Pretend we're not here. Just say the first name that comes into your head.'

Suddenly it was so obvious I felt like an idiot for not thinking of it before. 'I don't need to close my eyes,' I said, smiling.

You remember I told you, Ms Hiller, about when Sophie and I were kids, back when we were best friends, how we'd play faeries in the garden? We had Mad Hatter's tea parties with cupcakes and minty lemonade. Her faerie name was Ginger Parakeet. And mine?

'My name is Honeysuckle,' I declared. 'Honeysuckle Nightingale!'

Everyone at the table stared at me, silent, their mouths gaping open like so many goldfish.

'Really? That's the name you want?' Fred's voice was gravelly.

'What?' I asked, feeling suddenly, desperately insecure. 'Isn't that a good name?'

'It's just that Fred . . .' Ang started.

Golly, I thought. *If Ang is lost for words I really* must *have said the wrong thing.*

'I'm sorry, Clementine. It's just that, um, the name

Nightingale is already taken.' Fred clicked his fob watch open and closed.

'Oh, well, that's all right,' I said. 'I can make up a new name. Who has the name Nightingale?'

'Ah, that would be me.' Fred smiled sheepishly, and bowed his head. 'Lord Franklin Nightingale at your service, my lady. But I don't mind if you keep the name, too.'

It felt like time had stopped, Ms Hiller. It felt like Fred had closed his fob watch and paused the world.

Fred and I had picked the *same last name*?

All at once, nothing else mattered. I didn't care if Fred wasn't cool enough; that Chelsea-Grace and Cleo *wouldn't approve*.

Fred is . . .

Quiet.

And strange.

And he talks oddly.

And he draws peculiar pictures sometimes.

And he wears *spats*.

Chelsea-Grace and Cleo would definitely think I'm crazy-cakes.

But maybe it doesn't matter now, what Chelsea-Grace and Cleo think. Maybe *they* were my stream, Ms Hiller.

Maybe I was always meant to turn against it.

I smiled as I looked around the table, at the motley little group assembled there. And they smiled back. And I felt welcome. I knew I'd made the right choice, joining this group. Choosing Fred.

I felt like I'd come home.

If I Could Say a Single Thing to Any Person of My Choosing, What Would It Be?
by Clementine Darcy

This is a difficult one, Ms H!

There are all the obvious ones:

* To Sam: Stop texting me. Stop putting notes in my locker. You're creepy, and I don't want to go out with you. And you know what? I have decided it *is* odd that *all* your friends *and your girlfriend* are Grade 9s. Is it because the Grade 10s know you're a plonker? Or because you like having a tribe of little minions to boss around? Well, you're *not the boss of me*, so . . . shoo.
* To Chelsea-Grace and Cleo: It wasn't my fault. I wish you'd believe me.
* To Fergus: I'm sorry I made you sad. Come back to us.
* To Sophie: You know, you don't need to be perfect *all the time.* Let your hair down sometime.

Every moment of every hour of every day, there is something that is the most important thing to me right now. And often that something is one of the items on my list above.

But I think that in *this exact moment*, the thing I most want to say to one person of my choosing is: *What do those words mean? The ones you just this very minute wrote down in your notebook? The ones that make my stomach scrunch, because I'm not sure I like what I think they mean?*

I want to say it to Fred. But I shouldn't have spied, from my desk, on his private writings. So I want to say it, but I can't.

What a weekend I had, Ms Hiller.

It's so big I'll have to break it up into several entries. I'll start with Friday. Because it comes first. And because it was the bad part of the weekend and I want to get the bad part over and done with.

It happened after school. I missed the bus.

Then I missed the second bus, and – as if I'd suddenly fallen into some strange space–time vortex – I somehow, in my flapping panic, managed to miss *the third and final bus, too.*

How did I achieve this? Even *I* am not completely sure, Ms Hiller.

In my defence, I don't often catch the bus. Mostly Dad picks me up. In the olden days of 3CD I'd sometimes walk to Cleo's house. But Dad is in the middle of an important assignment, and 3CD are, as you know, kaput. So public transport it is. Or would be, if I wasn't so utterly inept at it.

And so it was that I found myself alone in the ghost town that was the Burnie High car park, cold, hungry and cursing life, the universe and John Greenwood.

He's the dude who invented buses, Ms Hiller. I googled it.

Anyway, guess who happened to pull up beside me, right at that dark moment, in his bright-red pimped-up Subaru?

If you said it was Fred Paul, you haven't really been paying attention.

In fact, even if Fred was old enough to have his Ps, I can't imagine him driving a car. I *can* imagine him piloting an airship, or pedalling a penny-farthing, or riding in a horse and carriage. But even if he did drive, do you really think he'd be seen dead in a red sportscar?

Of course it was Sam Peterswalds.

He rolled down his electric window and said, 'Need a lift, Clem?'

And, in a fit of bus-timetable-induced post-traumatic stress – despite all the messages he'd sent, asking if I want to hang out, go to the movies, drink vodkas in his garage, go to the beach, go to heaven in the back seat of his Cadillac (okay I made the last one up) – idiotically, I said yes. Sometimes, when we're cold and hungry and stressed, the current in the stream seems particularly strong. Sometimes, it carries us away . . .

'Buckle up, gorgeous,' Sam said, before reaching over and *doing it for me.*

'Thanks. I could have done that myself.'

'No worries. I'm a gentleman,' he said.

I almost vomited.

'So, what's a sexy girl like you doing all alone in a ghetto like this?' Sam pressed 'play' on his car stereo. Thumping R'n'B blared out, so loudly I thought my eardrums might rupture.

(*Down and dirty wid ma bitch in da club, yo, pimpin' it up 'til the break o' dawn, yo*, went the song. Shakespeare it was not. It was *definitely* no Jimmy Buffett.)

'Bit loud, isn't it?' I yelled.

(. . . *da club, yo* . . .)

'This shit's gotta be listened to loud!' Sam hollered back.

(. . . *bitch.*)

What a gentleman.

We turned out of the school driveway and onto the Bass Highway. 'Do you even know where I live?'

'West Wynyard, baby.'

(How did he know that?)

'Where do *you* live?'

I was getting tired of having to yell everything.

'Ridgley,' Sam yelled back, oblivious.

'But that's in THE OPPOSITE DIRECTION!' I just about screamed at him.

He seemed to get the message that time. He turned the volume down a bit. 'That's okay. We're not going straight home anyway.'

My palms began to sweat. 'What?'

He gave me his special smile. The Cheshire Cat one. 'I thought we might go for a drive. I've wanted to hang out with you for ages, Clem. Ever since that night when your mate Chelsea-Grace went mental. And I know you've been feeling awkward about it, because of her, but you don't need to worry. She's way too immature for me, and besides, she got with that skater fag Kerrard Stead at Dan Francombe's party, so it's not like she's Little Miss Sweet and Innocent. You don't need to feel bad.'

Sam stopped talking then, and started singing along with the horrible music. He tapped on the steering wheel and nodded his head.

'Uh, Sam?'

'Yes, beautiful?'

'I'm not going anywhere with you. You're taking me home.'

He didn't reply.

'Sam?'

No answer.

'SAM. ARE WE CLEAR?'

He resumed his singing. He was starting to freak me out now. But we *were* heading towards my place. I told myself to calm down.

A few minutes later, however, he took a turn that was *not* in the direction of my house. My stomach lurched sickeningly.

I forced myself to speak. 'Where are we going?' My voice

squeaked. 'Please, Sam, I don't . . . I *really* don't want to go anywhere with you. I just want to go home. You can drop me in town if you want. I'll catch a town bus to Wynyard from there.'

'I told you, it's okay,' said Sam. 'I don't mind driving you home. And we're not going far. Just . . . here, in fact.' He turned the car again, into the street that leads to Cam River Reserve.

'I don't want to go to the park, Sam,' I protested. 'I need to go—'

I was panicking, Ms Hiller. I was scared. Sam Peterswalds is strong. He plays lots of sport. He has big muscles. And I may not be a fragile waif, but I *don't* have muscles. And I can't run fast, despite Cleo and Chelsea-Grace's best efforts.

I hated myself for wishing it, but I wanted Fred Paul to arrive at that moment, on a white horse, to save me.

Preferably with a big sword.

I wished I could protect myself. But I wasn't sure I could.

Sam pulled into the gravel car park and killed the ignition.

My heart was thudding.

I didn't want to be by the Cam River, pretty as it was. I didn't want to be anywhere, alone, with Sam Peterswalds. I didn't want him reaching over and unbuckling my seatbelt – but he did.

'Sam, I'm not kidding. I want to go home. Please let me go home. My parents are expecting me—'

'So I'll come in and tell them I whisked you away and it's all my fault, and they'll be won over by how romantic I am. And . . . what's the word? Lecherous.'

I think he probably meant 'chivalrous', but his Freudian slip was much more apt. I would have laughed, if I wasn't so scared.

'Come on, Clem. You know you're hanging out for it. Come on, baby. You know you want me.' Sam leaned towards me, his face nuzzling into my neck. And then I felt a hot, flicking wetness.

He was *licking me.*

I was frozen. It didn't feel *real.*

He put his lips on my lips, and he pushed his tongue inside.

It was my first kiss, Ms Hiller.

I shoved him away.

'What the— I *know* you want it,' he hissed at me, looking in turn startled and then furious. 'You fat girls. You're always desperate for it.'

And Ms Hiller, at that moment, something *snapped.*

Something inside me went: *Enough.*

A voice in my head yelled: *Are you really going to let him say that, Clementine Darcy? Are you really going to let him* do *that?*

And, from some deep, dark place within me, it came: A long, loud, bloodcurdling scream. Followed by a bite. On his neck. I know! How very *Twilight* of me!

It turned out that I didn't need Fred Paul after all. I *could* protect myself!

'Ow!' Sam cried. 'What the hell? You bitch!'

There was a tap at the window, on my side of the car, and we both jumped. A man was standing outside. 'Are you okay, love?' he called through the glass.

I recognised him. Mr Vaskos, the pharmacist from the chemist in Wynyard. He's Tansy Vaskos's dad. She does dancing with Cleo.

I pushed the door open, nearly concussing Mr Vaskos in the process, and stumbled out of the car. 'Take me home, please,' I begged him.

'Do you need me to call the police?' he asked, peering in at

Sam. I shook my head violently. He put his arm around me. 'Hey,' he said, pointing at Sam. 'What do you think y—'

Sam had reached over to pull the passenger door shut. He shook his head at me in disgust. Then he hit the accelerator, and sped away.

'Hey!' Mr Vaskos yelled, impotently, in his wake.

'Please just take me home,' I said quietly.

And so Mr Vaskos drove me to Wynyard, in his white Camry with his beagle in the back, and I cried the whole time, and he didn't ask me any more questions, which I appreciated. When we pulled into our driveway, though, he turned to me and said, 'I'm going to have to come in and talk to your parents. You understand that, right?'

I nodded.

Mr Vaskos came inside, and I went to my room, so I didn't hear what he said to Mum and Dad. After a while, they appeared at my bedroom door.

They sat with me. They didn't ask me anything. They didn't prod. They let me cry.

'Can I come in?'

Sophie sat quietly on the bed beside me. 'What happened, Clemmie?'

Dad looked at me and I nodded. When he'd finished telling Mr Vaskos's story, Sophie growled, 'That little *bastard*.'

Not Mr Vaskos's story. *My* story. Though it didn't feel like mine at all. It felt as if it had happened to someone else.

'Are you going to the police?' Soph asked. 'Are you going to—'

She was interrupted by the sound of a door, down the hallway, clicking open.

We all fell silent, barely breathing, as we listened to the sound of footsteps, padding towards us up the hallway.

'Who hurt you?' asked Fergus.

Dear Clementine,

I was very sorry to hear of your ordeal on Friday night.

I am glad you felt secure enough in this environment to reveal this information to me.

However, I must inform you that I am obliged, in my role as your teacher, to disclose the details of what happened to you on Friday night to the relevant authorities, if you have not done so yourself. Based on what you told me, I think the young man in question did something to you that was very wrong. I think it must be reported. At the very least, he took you somewhere without your consent. And he should not have kissed you without your consent, either. You do know that, Clementine?

Please see me after class or, if you would prefer, simply write me a note.

I am proud of you for having the courage to tell me, and your parents, about this incident.

Ms Hiller

Dear Ms Hiller,

I'm sorry. I shouldn't have left my last entry on such a cliff-hanger. I should have told you how things resolved. I made you worry, and that was wrong of me.

I thought I might cry in class if I wrote any more. I'll tell you the rest now.

We did call the police, Ms Hiller.

Fergus saw how upset I was. He looked me in the eye, for the first time in a year. 'You need to let Dad make the call,' he said. 'It's important. Okay, Clem?'

I'm not sure I would have agreed, if anyone else had asked.

Fergus held me tightly, and Sophie rubbed my back, and I felt good that Dad was calling. I know there are many girls who have things like this happen to them – and even *worse* things – and don't tell.

I'm glad I told.

I'm glad Fergus had the strength to make me.

The police came, and they took my statement, and then they asked if I wanted to press charges.

They said it was my choice.

I said I didn't want to.

And I hope this doesn't make you less proud of me, Ms Hiller, but I *couldn't* do it.

It's not because Sam's popular and I'm scared of him, if that's what you think. It's more that I wanted it to end. I wanted the police to know what he'd done, but I didn't want to go to court. I didn't want it to be in the papers. My family had enough to deal with.

I wanted to shut the door on it and make it go away.

I said that, and Fergus got a funny look on his face and didn't say anything in return.

The police told me I could change my mind.

I might still change my mind.

After they left, Fergus grew quiet and then, after a while, he said he needed to lie down.

'Can you please stay?' I knew I sounded desperate. I *was* desperate. 'Fergus, I don't want you to go back in there and not come out.'

'Clem.' Dad's voice was gentle, but there was a hint of warning.

'It's okay, Dad,' said Fergus. He took my hand. 'I'm sorry, Clem. I'll try harder. I promise.'

And then he left. I burst into tears again. I really thought I'd brought him back. For good. But he went back to his room.

After that, Mum and Dad asked if I wanted to get a movie, or takeaways, or both. I knew they were trying to cheer me up, but I didn't feel like it. I felt like being alone. I told them I was fine; that I was just going to stay in my room and do some writing.

I wrote until my fingers were sore. I wrote until my eyelids sagged. And it did help, but I was still angry and confused. I was still sad.

The next morning, though, Fergus came down to breakfast. He didn't say much, and he didn't eat much. But he was there. And, before he went back to his room, he said, 'Dad, I wouldn't mind if you called that Elizabeth lady again. I'd talk to her.'

I had a big breakfast, because I hadn't eaten any tea on Friday night – a bowl of Sultana Bran with soy milk, and a banana smoothie, and a breakfast bar.

Then I remembered I was supposed to be at the steampunk ball in a few hours. And my entire breakfast came to life and began a particularly dramatic dance in my belly.

'Clemmie, I'm going to stay home today,' said Soph. 'I was going to go out to . . . um, Pilates, but I know you and Cleo and Chelsea-Grace aren't getting along, and I'm worried about you being lonely, so I want to be here with you.'

I wrapped my skinny, shiny sister tightly in my arms. I knew it was a big deal for her, to offer to change her routine. 'You should go to Pilates. You enjoy it, and I actually have plans. But thank you.'

'Plans?' Sophie arched a perfectly plucked eyebrow. 'Have you made up with 3CD?'

I shook my head. 'Plans with other friends. New friends.'

Sophie nodded. 'I think that's a good thing, Clem. A really good thing. I love Cleo and Chels – they're like little sisters to me. But I think it's healthy that you're branching out in new directions.'

'Even if those new directions involve a corset and a croquet mallet?' I asked, expecting Soph to look at me as if I'd lost my marbles.

'Steampunk society?' she said.

'How did you know?' I gasped.

'The little sister of one of the girls in my law study group is in it,' she said. 'Angharad, I think her name is? Her sister Arwen told me about it, and I think it sounds interesting. I was considering joining myself, except with sport and study and Pilates, I don't have the time for another hobby right now. I'm thrilled that you're doing it, though, Clem. You'll have fun.'

And I did, Ms Hiller.

But I'll tell you about that tomorrow.

The Steampunk Ball by Clementine Darcy

Before the ball, I went over to Gemma's house. Dad drove me, because she lives in Somerset, and when he stopped the car, instead of saying 'Have fun!' like he usually would, he reached over and gave me a huge hug.

'I love you, possum.' His eyes were shining with tears.

'I love you too, Dad,' I said softly, my own eyes prickling.

Once I'd left the car, my heart began to race. I was both excited and terrified. Before this, the only 'ball' I'd attended was my Grade 6 leavers' dinner, with Harry Potter theme!

Gemma's mum led me through the house and let me out the back, where Lucy, Ang and Gemma were already sitting on the far side of the large, neat garden at a white lacework table. They had on their steampunk outfits and were drinking some kind of greenish-yellow drink from tall glasses.

'Hey!' Gemma called, waving with her free hand (the other was busy texting). 'Come and join us. We're having elder-flower cordial!'

As I approached, I saw them squinting and peering at me. When I got close, they all leapt up (as best as one *can* leap in a corseted gown). 'No!' they shouted. 'Stop! Hold on!'

I raised my hands in the air. 'What?' I cried. 'You said to join you!'

'Yes, and then as you came closer, we realised what you're wearing!' Ang cried gustily, her blonde curls bouncing madly as she jumped up and down on the spot.

'What?' I asked, looking down at my long floral skirt and denim jacket. 'What's wrong with it? I know I'll have to get changed, but we can do that later, can't—'

'Not later. Now.' Gemma's hands were on her waist (as opposed to her hips, which were completely obscured beneath the beginnings of an enormously flouncy skirt). 'You have to get changed *now.* You can't attend a pre-ball garden party dressed like a peasant.'

'Come on guys, let Clem sit down and catch her breath first,' Lucy interjected quietly. She was the only one not wearing a corset. Instead, she had on black knickerbockers, like the ones Fred sometimes wears, and a tight red velvet blazer with bows on the sleeves. She wore a top hat on her head and shiny black Mary Janes on her feet. Her lips were the colour of her blazer. She looked spectacular.

I hovered awkwardly for a moment, until Ang pulled out a chair and patted it enthusiastically. 'Do join us, milady,' she said, winking, and poured me a cordial.

Gemma snorted in amusement. 'Sorry about that, Clem. I get excited about the outfits. How are you? How's your weekend been so far?'

Her question crushed my excitement like a delicate Victorian jelly beneath a crashing airship. Suddenly all I could think about was the night before – how awful it had been.

I hesitated. If it had been Cleo or Chelsea-Grace, I probably would have lied – said I'd spent the weekend reading and watching Important and Serious Documentaries on the history of English grammar (and watched their eyes glaze over). But I didn't feel like lying to my new steampunk friends. And I knew they wouldn't judge me. So I told the truth.

When I'd finished my story, Gemma simply sat there for a few moments, her eyes wide and unblinking, her mouth hanging open. Then, her eyes narrowed. 'I'll freaking kill him,' she growled.

'Me, too,' said Lucy. She said it with characteristic quietness, but genuine menace.

'And I'll help,' exclaimed Ang, easing herself out of her chair and shuffling forward. I think she was aiming for a determined stride, but it's hard to stride through several layers of tulle and crinoline. When she finally covered the metre or so between our chairs, she gave me a big hug. 'Seriously, who does he think he is? What an absolute creep! Who acts like that? We are so totally going to do something really, really nasty to him, possibly involving hooking up some sort of steam-powered stabby device to his testic—'

'But first,' Gemma interrupted, 'we're going to make you look so damn *smokin'* that Fred Paul will fall even more madly in love with you.'

'Yeah!' Ang punched a fist into her palm. 'He can show you what a real man is. This Sam Peterswalds isn't a man. He's not even a *mouse*. He's like . . . a rotten piece of fish that's been eaten by a dog and then regurgitated and stuffed into one of Noel's smelly socks and left in the sun for a week, and then pooed on. By an elephant. I don't want you to think about him even once at the ball, right? Today you're Honeysuckle Nightingale, not Clementine Darcy, and Honeysuckle Nightingale is going to be fabulous and not waste a millisecond of her energy thinking about rotten-vomited-fish-in-a-sock-with-poo-on-it guy. Okay?'

'Yes. But—'

'No buts! Come. We will transform you.' Gemma grabbed me by the arm.

And they did. At twelve, I was Clementine Darcy, average-looking twenty-first-century teenager. By one-fifteen, I was

Honeysuckle Nightingale, enchanting lady of the nineteenth century. Complete with gloves. And a parasol. And little ringlets, and a corset I was quite sure qualified as a human rights abuse.

Oh, and did I mention the pink bustle that made me look as though I had a cupcake on my bottom? That was different.

It was odd looking at myself in the mirror. I wasn't an awkward teenager anymore. But I was still Clementine. In fact, I think I was more Clementine than I had ever been before.

I think Fred Paul liked it, too, Ms H.

When we arrived at Natone Football Club, Fred came to 'escort us from our carriage' (which was actually Gemma's dad's Prius). He looked at me as if I was the only girl in the car park.

As if I was the only girl in the *world*.

He took my hand. 'I know I shouldn't say this – again – but you do look stunningly beautiful tonight, Lady Nightingale.'

'Why shouldn't you say it, er, Lord Nightingale?' I asked.

'Because you're . . . It's simply that . . . I'm me. And you're you.' Fred opened his watch and snapped it shut again.

'What am I?' I asked as we walked inside the club building. 'What—' I nearly dropped my parasol. 'Holy freaking *cannoli*.'

For a moment I forgot all about Fred and what he'd said, as I gazed around at the utter *craziness* that was the hall. Granted, I had never been to Natone Football Club before, but I felt quite sure that when the Magpies came here for their post-match Boagsies, they didn't sit on polished wooden chairs, at wrought-iron tables . . . or gaze around at framed antique maps and specimen jars full of dead insects and butterflies . . . or enjoy a centrepiece model of a Victorian-era dirigible (that's a whopping big airship, for you laypeople out there).

'It's . . . astonishing,' I said. 'Who created it?'

'Well, it was actually me this time,' said Fred. 'We take turns decorating.'

'You did all this?' I was breathless.

'Yes. I don't really have much of a life apart from school and steampunk.' He shrugged. 'I have the time.'

Fred showed me to my chair, beside his, and pulled it out for me.

'My lady,' he said.

'Why thank you, kind sir,' I replied.

The next hour, Ms Hiller, was one of the most wondrous and strange of my entire life.

After everyone was seated, a woman took the stage. She was dressed completely in black, in knickerbockers and a blazer like Lucy. She had a moustache drawn on her lip in what looked like black liquid eyeliner, and her eyebrows had been shaved and drawn back on as curlicues. Beneath her bowler hat, her hair – dyed an inky blue – was cut short and styled into little pin-curls around her face. When she spoke, she had a French accent. I'm quite sure it was fake, but it sounded fabulous.

'Welcome, fellow steampunkers!' she said, spreading her arms wide. 'I am Madame le Chat, and it is my duty to welcome you to a night of magic, mystery and wonder. Welcome to the place you were always meant to be. Welcome to a universe of Babbage Engines and curly wolves, of scuttlebutt and fogles, of cogs and gears and pulleys and levers that work *magic* when they move! Of illusion and trickery and all manner of ocular surprise and intrigue!'

'Is she speaking English?' I whispered to Fred.

'No,' he whispered back, chuckling. 'She's speaking steampunk.'

'To all of you who have felt that this decade, or indeed this *century*, is not when you were meant to live . . .' Madame le Chat went on. 'To all of you who feel that life is moving too rapidly . . . I say it is not *you* who are wrong in your way of living. It is everyone else. And they are missing out! For this – all of this – is only for you special people. This—'

'Oh, will you never close that flapping mouth of yours, woman?'

My head whipped around. A man was stalking towards Madame le Chat. He held a walking stick and wore a top hat. He had a waxed moustache, a pointy goatee, and thick mutton-chop sideburns. He spoke with a French accent, too, and he was striding towards Madame le Chat as if he intended to murder her.

'What's going on?' I asked Fred. This was thrilling!

'Oh, that's John. I mean, Jean. *Jean le Chat.* He's her husband. In real life and in BSS, although in real life their surname is Alston. In real life, they're very . . . romantic. In the show they hate each other. It's highly amusing to watch.'

'Not you again!' Madame le Chat snarled, rounding on 'Jean'. 'How many times must I tell you, this is *my* show. This is *my* ball. This is—'

Jean felt inside the pocket of his black velvet jacket and extracted a small, shiny silver pistol. 'Not for very much longer, my pretty!' he declared.

I expected Madame le Chat to scream and run, but instead she reached inside her coat and pulled out a *rifle.* (I have no idea how it fit in there either, Ms Hiller!) 'That is what you think, le Chat!' she growled.

Then, Jean le Chat *did* scream – with magnificent melodrama – and ran from the hall, with Madame le Chat in hot pursuit. As she exited the room (into the footy club change rooms), she bellowed, 'Let the frivolities begin!'

What happened next was even more incredible. A string of dancing girls, like a cancan line at the Moulin Rouge, snaked their way into the room and performed a dance for us.

Then an older man with long silver hair and a goatee that almost reached his chest rose from his seat and challenged any gentleperson in the room to a duel. To my surprise, Fred Paul stood and accepted the dare. They faced off with long silver duelling swords and . . . Fred won!

As everyone clapped and cheered, he marched straight over to me. He took my hand and kissed it, and everyone whooped and whistled.

It was all very fun.

And quite sexy, too!

Then the food came out. And oh, the *food*, Ms Hiller! I am spoiled for all other food for the rest of my life. There was roast beef and stuffed quails and oysters and pies and herrings and glazed vegetables, and for dessert there were elaborate jelly creations and steamed pudding and amazing confections I have no idea *what* to call, but they were *delicious*.

After dinner, a cricket match was set up for the boys, and a game of croquet for the girls. Yes, I do know the gender-segregation is ridiculous, Ms Hiller. And yes, some of the girls – including Lucy – revolted and played cricket, but it kind of seemed okay, because it was old-fashioned and all a bit silly anyway. In the end I came second in the croquet, so maybe a touch of gender-segregation isn't *so* evil after all. I do think I could have been awesome at the cricket too, though . . .

Next there was *dancing*, and it was during the dancing – during a waltz with Fred Paul – that he . . . and I . . . kissed.

It wasn't a peck on the cheek. It wasn't a light little touch of his lips on mine. It was a huge, strong, wonderful, *passionate kiss*.

And then he moved his mouth, so that he was whispering in my ear. 'That was my first kiss,' he said. 'And it was magic.'

I thought about what Chelsea-Grace and Cleo had told me – that you should always make boys think it's not your first time; that it's being *experienced* that's sexy. And I thought, *no.* What Fred had just done was sexy. Being his first was sexy.

And I leaned over and I whispered, 'Me too.'

I don't think I was lying, Ms H. Sam did kiss me, but it was without my invitation and I didn't kiss him back. It didn't count.

So, that kiss with Fred Paul was my first.

And seeing the smile on his face after I told him that confirmed it for me: it was so much better than pretending I'd done it all before, as Chelsea-Grace or Cleo would have had me do. It just made everything feel extra special.

Fred pulled me into a tight hug. 'You really are beautiful, Miss Clementine Darcy,' he said.

And then he kissed me again.

There's more, Ms Hiller.

Nothing will top that kiss, but there is more news of note. News from the day after the ball. And the news is this: Cleo and I are speaking again.

It's strange. I spent so long wishing this would happen. Finally I started to accept it might not, and I was almost at peace with that, because I'd met Ang, Lucy and Gemma, and the steampunk boys, and they were so welcoming, so understanding. At the ball I found myself laughing and saying things around them that I'd never say in front of Chels or Cleo. I found myself being, well, *me*, and I liked it. I felt free and wild and comfortable in my skin. I hadn't felt that way around Cleo and Chelsea-Grace for a very long time.

I was happy, Ms Hiller, with my new friends. There was still a hole in my heart for 3CD, but it was a smaller hole. I was healing.

And then my phone rang.

It rang because of secrets badly kept, Ms Hiller. Because Tansy Vaskos's dad went home and told Mrs Vaskos what had happened, and Tansy Vaskos overheard and took Cleo aside after dancing on Sunday to ask if she knew what had happened, and if I was all right. Of course Cleo *hadn't* known what had happened, and she *didn't* know if I was all right, because we *weren't talking*.

So on Sunday night, just as I was sitting down with Soph to watch the new BBC costume drama we've both fallen in love with, I heard my phone ring. I leapt up and ran to my handbag, hoping, I confess, that it was Fred Paul. Even though

Fred Paul had already called me that day. And messaged three times. But it was not Fred Paul. It was Cleo.

'Hey,' she said. 'Are you busy? Can you talk?'

'No, I'm not busy.' I looked over at Soph apologetically.

Soph looked annoyed for a moment, and then sighed. 'I'll fill you in. But just so you know, I think the butler did it.'

'Hang on, I'll go upstairs,' I said to Cleo.

As I walked past Fergus's room, a crack of light filled me with gladness – he's started leaving his door open, Ms Hiller. A little bit.

'So. Hello,' I said, as I flopped onto my bed. 'Um, what's up?'

'What's up with me?' Cleo cried. 'What's up with you, more like!'

My first thought was that she must somehow have heard about me and Fred. I hated that I felt slightly sick to my stomach at the thought – sure, she wouldn't approve, but why did I even care?

'You can tell me about it,' Cleo said softly. 'I want you to talk to me about it. I'm sorry we weren't speaking when it happened. I'm sorry you couldn't call me Friday night.'

Friday night?

But I kissed Fred Paul Saturday. On *Friday* I was . . . Oh.

'Tansy told me,' Cleo went on. 'After dancing. I hope you don't mind. She overheard her mum and dad talking about it.'

'You're talking about Sam?' I asked.

'Did he really kidnap you? And assault you? Because that's what Tansy said . . .'

'Not exactly. But he took me someplace secluded without my consent. And then he kissed me. And I didn't want him to. So at that point, I bit him.'

'Why were you in the car with him in the first place?' Cleo asked.

'I missed my bus,' I said, feeling defensive. 'All the buses, actually. He offered to give me a lift home and I . . . I thought it would be all right. But then he said he wasn't *going* to take me home—' I felt tears pool in my eyes.

'You want me to come over?' asked Cleo.

'No, it's fine,' I said quickly.

I didn't feel like seeing Cleo, Ms Hiller. Before, I would have said 'yes' in a heartbeat – I wouldn't have been able to think of anything better than a visit from my best friend, to cheer me up. But something told me that unlike Ang, Lucy and Gemma, Cleo wouldn't be dreaming up crazy, outrageous revenge against Sam.

I was happy that she'd called. But I didn't want to be judged. I didn't want someone asking me, 'Why were you in the car?' Making me feel as if it was my fault.

'I . . . I promised Soph I'd spend time with her,' I said.

'Of course!' Cleo said. 'I'll see you tomorrow, though, right? I mean, you'll come and sit with us? With me and Chels? I'll call her now and tell her what happened. Don't worry, she won't be mad at you. She and Kerrard are together. Which is crazy. I never thought she'd be into someone like Kerrard. He's a bit feral. But he's cute, I guess, in a skater-boy sort of way. And I think she got sick of Sam always blowing her off, and talking about you. Looks like he really did have a thing for you the whole time. Not that that makes it okay.'

'No, it doesn't,' I agreed. *And why* would *Chelsea-Grace be mad at me?* I added silently. *I didn't do anything* wrong.

'I know, Clem. I'll call her. I'll explain everything. We really have missed you. I'll make sure Sam doesn't come anywhere near us anymore, too. I'll find a way. And, listen, Brent's still single. And he's a nice guy, Clemmie. I'll talk to him, too. He'll be so happy. It'll all work out. Just you see.'

'I don't—' I began, but Cleo wasn't listening.

'Don't worry, Clemmie. It'll all be okay. Tomorrow, everything can go back to normal.'

The thing is, Ms Hiller, I'm not at all sure that's good news.

On the Monday, Cleo led me to the group's new lunch spot, in the quad.

She'd grabbed me by the arm after the bell rang, and I just . . . went.

Like a dead fish.

That day. And the next, and the next . . .

The group has expanded to include Todd and Kerrard, and Rosalinde's new boyfriend, Luke, an arty type who's mates with Kerrard. And Brent, who at first I thought was only tagging along with Todd. Except he always seems to sit next to me. And Cleo's right. He is nice. But he's not *Fred*.

Chelsea-Grace has forgiven me. Not that I think I need to be forgiven. Not that anything that happened with Sam was in any way my fault.

What Gemma said to me, in her garden before the ball, was: 'He's a creepy sleaze, always preying on the Grade 9 girls. He's an icky, misogynistic pervert. Anybody can see that. Your friends should have seen that, right back when he first hit on you at that restaurant. They should have known it wasn't your fault. None of this is your fault.'

What Chelsea-Grace said was: 'It's all over, hon. I forgive you totally. I'm so glad we're friends again.'

Ms Hiller, I'm glad we're friends again, but I don't want to be forgiven. There's nothing to forgive.

And also, I miss hanging out with Fred, under the cider gum.

I told him that the fight was over. He said, 'I'll give you some space, then. To fix things with your friends?'

'Thank you,' I said. 'But it doesn't mean I wouldn't prefer to be—'

'I know,' he said, smiling. 'I'd prefer that, too. But you need to do this, don't you?'

I nodded. 'Yes.'

'We'll meet again one day beneath the cider gum,' he said. And then he kissed me again.

And I don't know what we are now, Ms Hiller. I don't know if we're boyfriend and girlfriend. I don't know if he is writing about me in his exercise book, while I write about him.

I hope so.

I hope that's the *sort* of thing he's writing, at least, Ms Hiller. I hope he's not writing the sort of words I accidentally saw him write the other day.

I know I can ask him anything, but right now it seems as if everything else in my life is too scary and confusing, and I feel as if I can't take on any more.

It's not brave of me, Ms Hiller. It's nothing like the Clementine I want to be, but I'm going to wait a little while longer before I ask about those words. I want a few more small moments that are only happy.

What I Did Last Night by Clementine Darcy

Last night, I got a lift home with Fred Paul. On his bicycle.

It's not an ordinary bicycle, Ms H. It's an *antique* bicycle, of course, with a sidecar that's just perfect for romantic cycling!

It wasn't the fastest way to get home, but it was without a doubt the best trip between Cooee and Wynyard that I've ever experienced. We cycled by the sea, with the salty air on our faces and the winter sun warming the backs of our heads. The sky was a hazy sort of blue, and the breeze smelled like dusk and sand and freedom. When we got to Wynyard, Fred said, 'Do you want to go straight to your home, or would you like to park somewhere and simply . . . simply spend some time together first?'

'I'd like to spend some time together,' I said without hesitation.

So we turned off before the main street of Wynyard, into the little park with the duck pond. Fred chained up his bike and then, from the compartment under my seat, he pulled out his little wicker basket and red picnic blanket.

'I was hoping you'd decide upon the second option,' he explained when he saw the surprised look on my face.

'I'm very glad I went for the second option,' I said, smiling.

We had a gorgeous picnic together, down by the water. Fred had packed homemade pikelets and jam and cream, and grapes, and shortbread fingers, and a small bottle of elder-flower cordial, and we ate and talked, and then we kissed a bit, and just as the sun was starting to set and make dancing mermaids on the water's surface, Fred turned to me and said, 'Clem, would you like to . . . uh . . . I don't quite know how to put it. If we were in Victorian times, I suppose I'd ask if you would like to *step out with me*. Now, I expect I should ask if you'd . . .' He cleared his throat. 'Will you be my girlfriend?'

He pulled out his fob watch and began to flick it open and closed. I put my hand over his, stopping him.

'Yes,' I said. 'I'd love that.'

'Good.' Fred breathed out shakily. 'I was hoping you'd say that. It will make the whole being married at BSS thing so much less embarrassing.'

'Hold on. I didn't know I was agreeing to be your wife,' I said, grinning at him. 'I think I'm a bit young for that kind of commitment.'

'Oh, me too!' Fred kissed me on the cheek. 'But maybe, at BSS, it might be fun to, well, pretend. Gemma and Noel pretend to be betrothed, so we wouldn't be the first. Liam and Josh would *like* to pretend to be married, but it wasn't quite the done thing in Victorian society for two men to do that. Sadly, not much has changed. We could, of course, refuse to be married to support their cause, but since we share a surname, if we weren't married we'd have to be brother and sister, and that would make the, uh, *kissing* just a smidgen inappropriate.'

'We'll stage a protest for marriage equality in the Victorian era to make it up to them,' I said. 'I'm sure Gemma would help. I would like to be married to you, at BSS. And in real life, I'll *step out* with you. *If* you'll give me just one more of those pikelets.'

'Done.'

'Fred—' I began, thinking I'd just say it; that I'd ask him straight out, right then and there, about the words I'd seen in his journal. But then . . .

He reached into the basket. And we kissed some more, and I didn't ask, and I *know* I was letting the stream carry me away but . . . it's such a nice stream, Ms Hiller, this one that Fred and I are in. So warm and cosy.

Later, when Fred and I arrived at my house, he said, 'Would you mind if I came in and introduced myself to your parents?'

'All right,' I agreed.

He helped me out of the sidecar and we walked, hand in hand, to the front door. Before I'd even got a chance to put my key in the lock, though, Dad flung the door open.

'Oh, thank God, Clem,' he said. 'We've been so worried. We thought you'd been—' He looked from me to Fred and back again. 'Who's this?' he said sharply.

'It's all right, Dad,' I said gently. 'This is Fred. He's—'

'Frederick Paul.' Fred extended his hand. 'I'm Clem's boyfriend.'

Dad nodded curtly. 'And where were you the Friday night before last?' he snapped, leaving Fred's hand hanging in the air.

'Dad!' I exclaimed. 'Fred wasn't . . . We weren't together then. And he doesn't know about it. He did nothing wrong.'

Dad's face softened. 'Okay. I'm sorry, young man. I've just been so worried.' He took Fred's hand, finally, and shook it. 'We must meet again, *properly*, very soon, all right?' He tilted his head, looking at Fred as if he was only now seeing him for the first time.

I bit my lip, waiting for his reaction to Fred's peculiar outfit. 'I like your hat,' he said finally, nodding at Fred's tartan flat cap. 'Had one quite like it during my university days. I must dig it out. I used to wear it with my *Man in Black* T-shirt. Ahh, Johnny Cash . . .' His eyes got a faraway look about them for a moment. 'Hmm. Anyway.' He turned to me. 'Elizabeth is here. With Fergus. Fergus has agreed to talk to her.'

'That's wonderful!' I said.

'Um, I should push off.' Fred's face was a picture of confusion. I didn't blame him. This couldn't have been what he'd expected when he offered to introduce himself to my parents.

'I'll see you tomorrow,' I said.

Fred gave a little bow. 'Very nice to meet you, Mr Darcy.'

'You too, Fred. You must come to dinner sometime. I'll wear my cap.'

'I'd like that,' said Fred.

After Dad went back inside, I turned to Fred and said, 'I'll explain.'

'When you're ready.' He kissed my cheek, removed his cap with a flourish, replaced it with his helmet, and rode off into the sunset.

I have the best boyfriend, Ms Hiller.

Inside, Mum and Soph were in the kitchen, cooking tea (actually, Sophie was cooking and Mum was having a glass of wine and being 'supportive'). The lounge-room door was shut.

Mum and Dad exchanged a parental 'look', which I deciphered to mean, *It's fine. I've dealt with it.*

'Fergus is talking with Elizabeth,' Mum said.

I nodded. 'Dad told me.'

'It's a good thing.' Sophie smiled. 'It's a positive step.'

'I'm going to go upstairs for a bit,' I said. Mum nodded.

'Tea will be ready in half an hour,' said Sophie. She kept stirring the pot. Her wrists looked so thin.

'All right,' I said, and I went off in the direction of my room. But when I got to the stairs, something stopped me.

I needed to know if Fergus was being fixed. I'd been a dead fish with Fred. I wouldn't be with Fergus. I wanted to know what he and Elizabeth were talking about. If it wasn't going well, maybe I could step in and help.

Fergus's voice was muffled through the heavy door, but I could still make it out. 'I don't feel sad,' he said. 'I don't feel anything.'

'That's normal,' Elizabeth said. 'That's what depression feels like. It's a misconception that it feels like sadness. Mostly, people say it feels more like numbness. Like you can't feel joy.'

'That's exactly it,' Fergus agreed. 'I feel like I'm wrapped up in cottonwool. Like everyone else in the world is outside a pane of glass. A frosted pane of glass. I can sort of hear them and sort of see them, and I can see that they're laughing and happy, or even *upset*. I can *see* that, but I can't . . . *touch* them. I can't understand. I can't feel happy with them or sad for them. I can't imagine ever feeling *anything* again.'

'How long have you felt like this, Fergus?'

There was a long pause. 'Ages.'

'Before you and your girlfriend broke up?'

'Ages before that. We broke up *because* I was like this.'

My breath caught in my throat. Fergus had been feeling like this for a long time? Before he and Alyssa split? Before he lost his job?

Before I made fun of him at breakfast?

'And it's why I lost my job, too. I stopped caring. It didn't seem important anymore. Elizabeth?'

'Yes, Fergus?'

'Will I ever care again, do you think? Will I ever kick this thing? Because I want to. I want to be a part of this family again. I want to look after Clem. After what happened to her . . . I know it's not my fault, but I feel responsible somehow. I'm her big brother. I should be protecting her! And Soph, too. Soph pretends like she's okay but the girl barely eats, Elizabeth. I want to be their big brother again. I want to be there for them.'

Tears streamed down my face. I didn't bother to wipe them away.

'Well, that's caring, isn't it?' said Elizabeth evenly. 'Do you feel there's glass between you and your sisters, when they're experiencing trauma?'

'Of course not!' Fergus protested. 'But I feel incapable of helping them. I don't have the energy.'

'This will end, Fergus. It might take time. You might even have to think about medication.'

'I don't want to, but I will. I want to make it up to them.'

'You need to make it up to yourself, Fergus.'

I pushed myself up from the floor then, and moved silently away from the door. I didn't want to listen anymore. This was private, between Fergus and Elizabeth. I needed to let my brother fix himself.

An hour later, as the rest of us were eating dinner, the door to the lounge room opened and Elizabeth emerged. She was wearing a long green velvet dress with red wooden beads, and her hair was twisted into a clip shaped like an Art Deco fan. She wore skull rings on her fingers and Doc Martens on her feet.

Elizabeth didn't fit on the north-west coast of Tasmania. She didn't dress as if she was from another time, like Fred, but she definitely dressed as if she was from another place. She didn't belong here, and yet she didn't appear to care. She belonged to herself, *with* herself. And that seemed to be enough.

She shut the door behind her and came over to us. 'It's early days,' she said. 'Fergus has a lot of guilt to work through.'

'Guilt? Why?' Dad's brow furrowed.

'He feels he's let you all down. He thinks he's failed you, because he lost his job and his girlfriend, and he's made you all worry about him for so long. His sense of shame is acute.'

'That's silly,' I said. 'He has nothing to feel guilty about. We love him. We'll always love him, no matter what.'

Elizabeth nodded. 'I think that's part of the problem, actually – which isn't your fault. He feels as if he doesn't deserve your love. As if he can't live up to it. It's going to take him a while to accept your compassion and help again. I think it will be good for him if he's given a sense of purpose. If you need him; if he could help you. I think that would make a real difference.'

And so that's why, after Elizabeth left, I went into the lounge room and asked Fergus if he'd mind putting on a dinner party for our family, and my new boyfriend, Fred Paul.

Something I'm Worried About Right Now by Clementine Darcy

There are many things worrying me now, Ms H. Sometimes it feels as if my life is one big worry. There's Fergus's illness. There's Sophie's moodiness. There's Sam. There's Cleo and Chelsea-Grace and what's happening with 3CD.

And there's the future. That worries me too, Ms Hiller. What subjects will I do next year, in Grade 10? Will I truly study poetry at university, or end up doing something different? What if I don't get in? Do I even *really* want to go to university, or do I actually want to travel and write and let life teach me instead?

All of those things make me anxious, but right now there's one thing that's worrying me above everything else. It's about Fred. It happened before school. And I don't know what to do about it.

I was walking to class, alone temporarily because Cleo and Chelsea-Grace had popped to the toilet. Fred was standing at his locker with his back to me, dressed in his cape and his pinstriped pants and his shoes with spats, and there were three Grade 10 boys standing around him. As I walked past, I heard one of them say, 'What are you even doing here, you weird little psycho? You should have stayed where you came from. You're a freak.'

My blood froze. I couldn't believe someone had spoken

that way to Fred. I couldn't believe someone in *my school* had been so mean to him.

I wanted to stop. But I told Fred last night, after school, the whole story of what happened with Sam, Ms Hiller, and in this moment at the lockers today, I remembered the murderous look on his face; the way his jaw had tensed and he'd looked as if he was swallowing such fury; how, finally, he'd cleared his throat and said, 'Clementine, I wish to express . . . so many things. My sense of propriety prevents me. Needless to say, I wish to deck the bastard.' He'd told me then that he'd protect me from now on, no matter what. And so I didn't know today how he'd feel about *me* trying to protect *him*.

I was a bit scared as well, Ms Hiller, that if I intervened here I'd have to ask him about the other thing, too – what I'd seen him write in his journal; and that all of this together would pile on top of the little happy bubble we have and make it go *pop*.

So I just kept walking. He never knew I was there.

Should I have done things differently? I've never had a boyfriend before. I don't know what you're meant to do if someone is making them feel small.

In any case, I kept walking, and I still don't know if it was the stream carrying me along, or if I was swimming against it by not fighting when I wanted to. Sometimes it's hard to tell, Ms Hiller, if the stream is in control, or if I am.

Last night I went to Fish Frenzy again with some of the steampunkers.

Chels invited me over to her place, but I told her I'd promised Mum and Dad I'd stay home. I know it's wrong to lie to her and Cleo, Ms Hiller. They're trying to get me to go out with Brent, and I know all I need to do is tell them about Fred and they'll stop – I know I should be able to tell them about both Fred and BSS *anyway*, Brent or no Brent, because they're two really important things going on in my life right now.

But I can't. Everything is so good with Cleo and Chelsea-Grace now; it's as if our big fight never happened. I don't want to do anything to mess things up.

I'm going to the movies with them and their boyfriends on Saturday night. Brent will be there, but it won't be me and Brent *alone*. I'm doing it so that 3CD can be strong again. Fred knows I'm going – he knows Brent will be there, along with some other boys. He *doesn't* know Cleo and Chelsea-Grace are trying to set up Brent and me, though.

It's all too messy. So I'm writing all of that stuff out of my story, just for now, and making it all about me and Fred. And steampunk-themed dinner parties.

'Dad's crazily excited,' I told Fred as we waited for the others to arrive at Fish Frenzy. 'He found his hat, and he keeps talking in a strange accent. He thinks it's cockney, but it sounds more South African to me. Or maybe Spanish. It's hard to say.'

Fred laughed. 'I can't wait to hear it! I'm excited, too. It will be nice, getting to know your family.'

He put his arm around me, and I tried to forget about Saturday night, Brent, my splintery friendships with Chelsea-Grace and Cleo. I tried to forget about the things those boys in the hallway had said to Fred, too. And the words. Those words. Fred's words. The ones I'm rubbing out in my mind. The ones that keep rewriting themselves.

After a while, I did forget. Because everything was so lovely.

We chatted about our favourite classic steampunk books, and argued over who was the best Sherlock Holmes. I said Robert Downey Junior, and Fred accused me of having a crush on him and being biased, and, well, it all led to a tickle fight. Naturally.

When Ang, Gemma and Lucy arrived, they just about fell over themselves attempting to sound out whether I was feeling okay without letting on to Fred what had happened with Sam, until he let them know that he knew, and we were all able to freely revisit our ideas for revenge together. (After he'd been pooed on by an elephant, it turned out that Sam would be shot out of a cannon, made to eat cabbage cupcakes, and then sent to Timbuktu.) I know we won't enact any of these ideas, of course, but it was therapeutic to talk about it.

Eventually the conversation took on a more serious note, and I explained to them that in truth I'm not really the revenge type, but rather more of the 'let it go' type, a la Jimmy Buffett. I may always want to try to fix things, but revenge doesn't feel to me like fixing – it feels like ripping and tearing and cutting and *hurting* even more. I'd prefer to focus on my friends, my family; on Fergus getting better – I told them about him, too; on moving on. I was trying very hard not to worry about what I would do when I next bumped into Sam at school, which hadn't happened yet.

I may have only known them a few weeks, but all four of

them listened so intently and respectfully as I told them that, Ms Hiller. It felt as though they'd do anything for me.

I'd do anything for them, too. It feels as if I've known them forever.

And they love Fred, too, Ms Hiller. You can really tell that they care. I wondered if they'd know the meaning of the words Fred wrote. For a little while I was almost tempted to ask them. But then I realised that was the cowardly option. And I'd decided to be brave.

It was after dinner. The others had gone. Fred and I were walking along Marine Terrace, holding hands. 'Fred?' I said, tentatively.

'What, Clem?' He leaned over and kissed me on the cheek.

I almost didn't ask then, Ms H, because the kiss was so nice and it would have been easy to get distracted by it, but I knew I had to do it.

'Fred, I saw something.'

'Hmm?' Fred said, and waited for me to go on.

So I did.

'Um, accidentally. In class, we were writing in our journals, for Ms Hiller, and I was just watching the back of your head – in a not-creepy way, I promise – and I saw the heading you wrote for one of your entries. It said, *I try not to think of what happened back then, because thinking of it is like dying inside, all over again.* You were talking about what happened in Sydney, weren't you?'

When Fred didn't reply immediately, I steamrolled on. 'And, um, don't get angry, Fred, but I heard those boys in the hallway the other day. They were so awful to you, and you didn't even respond. It's connected, isn't it?'

Fred didn't get angry, Ms Hiller. He didn't become cold and distant. He didn't walk away. He stopped, and he turned to me, and he said, 'Things weren't so great at my old school, Clem. That's all. Those boys at the locker? That's nothing on what I had to put up with back home. You might think it would be better in the big city, but it's not. Back in Sydney, I got picked on big-time. By this one group of boys in particular. About my hair, and my clothes – even though they were much more 'normal' back then – and for daydreaming in class, and even the way I walk. Apparently I walk like a giraffe.'

'I never noticed,' I said gently.

Fred smiled. 'That's probably because it isn't true. Those boys had just decided to pick on me, come what may. And I knew that. But still, every day was a nightmare. Every day I wanted to disappear. Every day I felt like I was dying inside – that's what I meant in my journal. That's all. Those kids were bastards.'

'You don't mind talking about it?' I asked.

Fred shook his head. 'Not with you.' He swallowed. 'I was always different. I never wore the right clothes, or talked the way other kids did. At home, that was okay. My mum's always encouraged me to be myself. Without her, and her faith in me . . . heavens, I don't know where I'd be, Clem. She got me through, in Sydney. She never let me lose my belief that I was okay, a worthwhile person. But I still had bad days.

'At school, I'd hide in the library to get away from those guys. One day, they followed me there, and even the fabulous librarian couldn't stop them. So I did the thing I promised I'd never do . . . I hid in the toilets.'

'What's so bad about hiding in the toilets?' I asked, trying to understand.

Fred shook his head and smiled. 'You've got no idea of the stench that emanates from the toilets at an all-boys school. The levels of hygiene in Victorian London were infinitely better.

But anyway, it was in those hellish latrines that I found the quote that saved my soul. *I want to go ahead of Father Time with a scythe of my own*. It's HG Wells.'

'Gosh. At our school, the graffiti just says *Julia for Ryan forever*.'

Fred laughed. 'Sanitation levels notwithstanding, the school I went to was exceedingly upper crust. But the quote got me thinking, Clementine. About time, and about power, and about how none of us are really trapped by the time we're in and the circumstances we're faced with. We can choose to build our own time machines and make our own destinies. I let myself out of the toilets. I went straight home and told my mother that I wanted to leave. And so . . .' Fred spread his hands wide.

'And so now you're here, and you dress like this,' I said. 'Because of that quote?'

'Yes and no. I was inspired to read more HG Wells, and Jules Verne and, from them, I moved on to modern interpretations. And my love of steampunk was born. After that, it became something of an obsession. I realised those boys didn't have the power to influence my life. I realised I could change my life every day. Every day could be an adventure, and I wanted to live that adventure. And now I am. With you.'

Then he kissed me again. On the lips this time. And he hugged me. And I was glad I had asked. I was glad I knew more now about Fred. It only made me like him more.

Happy Monday, Ms Hiller.

Stop staring at me like that. I know I look strange. And I'm grinning like a loon. But I'm about to explain everything.

Are you curious?

It turned out that my decision to go to the movies with the girls and Brent on Saturday night was not the most sensible one I'd ever made. In fact, as it happens, it was one of the most *rotten* decisions of my entire life.

We met up beforehand at Himalaya Curry, which was a definite step up from the noodle place. Cleo told me Brent had suggested it. Because he thought I might like it. That should have been my first clue that I was not going to pull off pretending this was simply a movie night with friends.

The next clue was that when I arrived, everyone else was already present and there was only one spare seat – next to Brent. I took it. Maybe I shouldn't have, but Chels and Cleo seemed so happy. They had their boyfriends by their sides, teasing them and messing up their hair and doing all those bizarre things teenage boys do to show teenage girls they like them. And even though it wasn't the same sort of gentlemanly behaviour that Fred shows towards me, I could tell that Chelsea-Grace and Cleo liked it. This was courting, for them.

We girls talked about movies and music and clothes, while Kerrard explained some skatey moves to the jocks and the jocks tried to explain to Kerrard why skating was 'gay', and I got stuck into the jocks for using 'gay' as a derogatory term, and Chelsea-Grace was anxious until she realised the boys thought I was being funny.

I didn't have the energy to correct them. Plus, I was *almost* having a good time. It wasn't as fun and giddy and chaotic and *limitless* as spending time with the steampunk crowd, but it was nice. If only in a nostalgic way.

And then Sam Peterswalds walked in. With Chenoa.

Our entire table froze, which was when I realised that it wasn't just Cleo and Chelsea-Grace who knew about Sam.

It was everyone.

Their boyfriends. Brent. Probably everyone else from the group at school, too.

'It's okay, Clem.' Cleo squeezed my hand. 'It's okay.'

I saw Chenoa gesture towards the toilets. She kissed Sam on the cheek and walked away, pulling a lip gloss from her handbag.

When she was gone, Sam came over to our table.

'Hey guys,' he said to Todd and Kerrard.

Todd and Kerrard nodded silently back at Sam.

'What are you doing here, Sam?' Brent asked, his voice venomous.

'Just on a date with the missus, mate,' Sam replied.

'Well, you can piss off. Right now,' Brent spat.

Sam raised his hands. On the surface he was the same, cocky, self-assured Sam. But underneath, I could see he was shaken. 'Hey! Hey mate! Listen, I didn't mean to—'

'Did you not hear me? I said, you can just piss off. We all know what you did to Clementine. And it's not cool, *mate.* So if I were you, I'd just get out of here. And take your *poor bloody girlfriend* with you.'

Behind me, I heard someone suck in a breath. Chenoa had returned without any of us noticing.

'Brent,' I said, gesturing at her so he'd know she'd heard.

She nodded, dumbly. 'It's . . . okay,' she whispered.

Brent put his arm around my shoulder. 'Listen, Sam. I care about Clem. And you took her somewhere against her will; then, knowing full well she wasn't into you, you tried to jump her. None of us knows for sure what you might have done next if she hadn't protected herself. You're an arsehole, and we all know it now. Leave. Right now. Or I will punch your lights out. You might be older than us, and you might think you're top dog, but trust me, I will do some damage if you don't disappear.'

'Sam, I think we should go.' The expression on Chenoa's face was a mix of confusion, shock and horror.

'Yes, I think you should go. Now,' Brent repeated.

And that's when I reached up and pushed Brent's hand off my shoulder.

And stepped forward.

'I'm sorry you had to hear about all this in this way,' I said to Chenoa. 'None of this is your fault, just like what happened to me was not my fault. Sam is a nasty person, and I would advise you to dump him because, really, you deserve better. And because Sam does bad things to people who don't deserve it. Like me. He *did* try to kiss me. He *didn't* try to rape me, but it did seem like things might have been heading that way. I was really scared. Now you know that. You can choose to believe me or not.'

Chenoa just stared at me. She didn't say a word.

'I have friends who've offered to do brutal things to Sam in return,' I went on. 'Much as it would be fun to fill the boot of his car with rotten fish, I think the best thing I can do is tell you what he's really like, and then leave you to make an informed choice. So I'm telling you.'

I turned away from Chenoa's bug-eyed face and looked calmly at Sam.

'I have contacts in hospitality. I can get the fish. Just think about that if you're ever considering hurting any other girl. Okay? Now, please go.'

Sam nodded slowly. His face was ashen.

He took Chenoa's hand. As they walked out, Chenoa turned back and looked at me. There were tears in her eyes. But she didn't let go of his hand. She let him lead her away.

After the restaurant door slammed shut, everybody at our table turned and stared at me.

Brent put his arm around my shoulder again, and I knew he was just trying to protect me, but I don't need protecting.

I like it when *Fred* says he'll look after me, but only because . . . I'm falling in love with him, Ms Hiller.

I turned to Brent. 'I need to talk to you. Outside.'

We left the restaurant and stood by the entrance to the plaza, and he looked at me expectantly.

'I don't want to go out with you,' I said immediately.

I would have thought that was clear enough, wouldn't you, Ms H? Not for Brent, though. He put his arm around me, hugging me close. It wasn't sleazy and horrible, like when Sam had done it; instead, it felt almost comforting. But it wasn't right. He wasn't Fred.

'Did you hear me?' I asked.

Brent sighed and pulled away. 'Yeah, I did, Clem. I understand. I'm sorry. I'm not cool enough for you—'

'What!' I gaped at him. *He* wasn't cool enough for *me*? Was he joking?

'You're smart and funny and stuff,' he said, shrugging. 'And me? Well, I'm Sam's ugly, talentless friend. I get why you wouldn't want to go out with me.'

'No. No, no, no!' I shook my head. 'That's stupid! You're really attractive. And you're a lovely person. It's just that I already have a boyfriend.'

'What? But Cleo and Chelsea-Grace—'

'They don't know,' I interrupted.

'Why?'

'Because I'm a dead fish,' I sighed.

'Okay, I don't know what that means,' said Brent. 'But I guess I shouldn't be hugging you like I have been, then.'

'I guess not,' I agreed, smiling at him weakly.

'I'm happy for you, Clem,' said Brent, though he didn't exactly sound it. 'You deserve someone good. You're the best of those girls, you know? You're the most *real*.'

'Well, I think you're the best of those boys,' I said truthfully. 'Apart from when you say things are gay. You realise that's moronic, right?' Brent nodded sheepishly. I squeezed his hand. 'And I think you will find someone special. Someone who deserves you.'

'I hope so. I did really want *you*.'

'There are plenty more fish in the sea,' I said.

'You and your fish.' He grinned, and then gestured towards the restaurant. 'I'd better get back in. Are you coming?'

I shook my head. 'I think I'm going to go home and call my boyfriend. Tell Chels and Cleo I'll be in touch tomorrow.'

'This boyfriend of yours is one lucky guy.'

'I know,' I said.

Brent elbowed me gently. 'If he ever does wrong by you, I'll deck him.'

'Thanks,' I replied. I knew that it was Brent's way of being nice. Jocks are an unusual breed.

I sat down on a bench for a few minutes after he'd left, staring out at the sea. Then I headed for the taxi rank, so that I could go home and call Fred.

The trouble is, Ms Hiller, his friend Noel got in first.

♡

'I received a text from Noel,' Fred said the minute he picked up the phone.

'Really? Noel *texted*? Wonders will never cease.' I said it cheerfully. But something in Fred's voice troubled me. Something was wrong. 'What was the text about?' I prompted, when he didn't say anything back.

'It said that he saw you outside an Indian restaurant, with a *jock* who had his arm around you.' My chest tightened. 'I thought you were going to the movies with your friends.'

'I was,' I protested feebly. 'It wasn't . . . he wasn't—'

'It's okay, Clem,' Fred said, his voice even. 'A gentleman never pries. I guess you've had your fun with the geek now, right? You've gone back to someone on your own social level. I understand. We steampunkers know all about social classes. You're nobility. I'm . . . I'm a peasant. I'm lower class.'

'No! Fred, you're—'

'Clem, just don't worry about me. I can handle myself. I've been through much worse than this. I'll miss you, but I suppose you're where you belong now. With the beautiful people.'

'Fred—'

'I've got to go,' Fred said. 'I've started reading a fantastic book. I was going to lend it to you, but you've probably gone back to your bestsellers and blockbusters now, am I right? Your *popular* fiction? Good night, Clementine.'

Fred hung up. I threw my phone at the carpet and fell onto my bed, and I cried my eyes out.

At some point, I crawled under my doona. And for a long

time, I thought I'd stay there forever. All I wanted to do was hide, and wish it all away.

But then I remembered that funny look on Fergus's face when I'd said I wanted to shut the door on the bad stuff. And then *your* voice spoke in my head, and *it* said, *Don't be a dead fish, Clem. Swim against the stream.*

Since I started your class, I've grown fins and gills. I've battled against the currents. I've come a long way. But on Saturday night, I realised that it's time to take it further. It's time to push with my new fins and dive right over the waterfall.

And now I've done it, Ms Hiller. I've finally done it. Which is why I'm sitting here, in class today, looking like this.

As for the red paint?

I'm so sorry, but the bell just rang, so that I'll have to explain to you tomorrow.

You're confused, aren't you?

I don't blame you – I must have looked a sight on Monday, grinning away in my Victorian-era garb, covered in red paint.

I'll explain it to you the same way I tried to explain it to my dad when I arrived home in that state. He almost choked on his Tim Tam Slam. Hopefully you'll understand.

On Monday morning, I woke up feeling great. Because I'd finally decided I was going to jump off that waterfall. Or at the very least, open a parasol, Mary-Poppins-style, and float away.

All the way to Fred Paul.

I went to my wardrobe, and instead of pulling out my jeans and my Josh Ritter T-shirt, or my floral skirt and pink ribbed cardigan, I reached for an outfit I'd borrowed – not from Chelsea-Grace or Cleo, but from Angharad.

I reached for a long, shiny navy-blue skirt. I reached for a button-up dress coat in the same fabric, with a lace collar and cuffs that ended in a point, like diamonds. Then I pulled out a bustle, and a corset, silk stockings and suspenders, black lace-up boots and, finally, the pièce de résistance, a tall inky-black top hat with a shiny navy ribbon tied around it.

'Perfect,' I whispered to myself.

Soph was at the table when I came down for breakfast, nibbling at a bowl of muesli and yoghurt. When she saw me, her spoon paused in midair and a gooey glob plopped onto the tablecloth.

'Um, Clem, you look . . . astonishing, but isn't it a school day?'

I nodded and sat, as gracefully as I could manage, at the table. I poured cornflakes into a bowl and began chopping up a banana. Sophie continued to gawk. Finally she said, 'This is for the boy, isn't it?'

I nodded again.

'Brilliant,' said Sophie. I poured fresh, nutty soy milk over my cornflakes. 'You know people are going to stare,' she added.

'I know,' I said.

'You're so brave, Clem. I wish I was as brave as you are.'

'What do you mean?' I asked.

Sophie glared and jabbed a chunk of dried pineapple with her spoon. 'I'm in love with my Pilates instructor. Mason. I thought he liked me too, but it seems he has a girlfriend. I saw him with her yesterday, and she's just . . . normal. Kind of fat, with short hair and no make-up. I got my friend to ask Mason about her, and apparently Fiona – that's her name – works in a café. She's only a *waitress*. And I know I shouldn't think I'm better than she is because I'm studying law and I'm . . . *thin* and stuff, but dammit, Clem! I work so hard to look like this, and to do well at school. And in the end it all feels empty, because I wanted Mason and he's going out with plain old Fiona, and it made me think that no matter how hard I try, it's not going to make a difference. I can look as perfect as possible, and wear expensive clothes, and spend hours on my make-up, and study every single minute God gives me, and it won't make anybody love me. And I'm *miserable*.'

I stared at her, agape. Sure, Soph had been grumpy lately, but I'd thought she was stressed about school, or Fergus, or just annoyed with *me*. I'd never thought for a moment that my pretty, perfect sister was actually . . . sad.

But as I looked at her sharp cheekbones and tiny arms, I could finally see it. Sophie's whole *body* was sad.

Sophie sighed. 'I don't know why I try so hard anyway. Mum and Dad love me come what may, just like they love Fergus even though he's been . . . difficult, and they love *you* even though you can be strange at times.'

'I'm strange?' I asked, feeling curiously pleased.

'Clemmie, you're eating cornflakes in a Victorian gown,' she said, smiling. 'I don't mean it in a bad way. I'm jealous, actually. You're in love with the world, and you've got this big imagination, and you see *possibility* everywhere. I don't think life is that great anymore. I wish I was still like you. I wish we were still kids down at the bottom of the garden, being Ginger and Honeysuckle. I wish everything didn't feel so damn difficult. I wish I felt like what I was doing with my life was *exciting*. Why do I keep trying so hard, when I don't really care about any of it?'

'Don't you want to be a lawyer?' I asked.

Sophie shrugged. 'I don't know. I thought I did. I thought I wanted to be like Mum – she always seemed to be doing such exciting stuff, when she was away from us, and when I was a kid I spent half my life wishing I was already older so I could start being exactly like her. But now I'm actually studying it, I'm finding it fairly boring. I'm enjoying my photography elective a million times more than any of my law classes.'

'So why don't you study photography instead?' I asked as I scooped the last of the milky crumbs from the bottom of my bowl.

Sophie looked thoughtful. 'Hmm,' she murmured.

'And Soph,' I said gently. 'You're a bit *too* thin. Not in a good way. Be strong on the inside *and* the outside. If you're going to run after your dreams, you'll need the energy to do it.'

I don't know where that last line came from. It sounded

like something from a motivational poster, but it must have struck a chord with Sophie.

'I know,' she said quietly. 'It's time to stop, isn't it?'

'Stop what?' I asked.

'All of this.' She looked up and her eyes were shining. 'The stressing, the worrying, the need to control everything. Wanting the guy I can't have because he's in love with someone else. Stuff it, Clem, it's time to stop all of this.'

'You don't have to do it on your own. I'll help. We all will. Maybe even someone like Elizabeth, if you need it.'

'Yeah.' Sophie wiped at her wet cheek with the back of her hand. 'Maybe. Maybe that would be good. Maybe I need help.'

'I've got to go.' I pushed myself up awkwardly from the table. 'It'll all be fine, Soph. Please don't worry. I know I can't fix you – I tried to fix Fergus and that ended spectacularly badly – but I can help. I can be here for you. And, you know, Soph, don't worry about Mason the Pilates man. You'll find someone lovely. Someone who loves you exactly how you are.'

Sophie shrugged. 'Maybe I'll find them once I *work out* exactly who I am.'

I felt a pang in my heart for my sister. I have a feeling that Sophie will probably keep doing law, and that while one day she will without doubt meet a handsome, successful, *nice* man who will treat her like a princess, she might wind up marrying him because it's what she feels she should do, rather than what she actually wants . . .

I hope my feelings on this are wrong, Ms Hiller. I hope Sophie has the courage to swim against the stream.

On the bus to school, I ignored the other students as they stared and whispered and laughed. They could laugh all they wanted. I was glad to provide them with some amusement.

When we pulled into the Burnie High car park, I minced

my way off the bus with as much dignity as I could muster. I had a plan. I was going to, finally, fix *something.* I was going to patch up the hole in the bubble of me and Fred. And I was going to do it with the aid of poetry and steampunk. The trouble was, I hadn't banked on being confronted, as I alighted the bus, with the other two members of 3CD.

'What on earth are you wearing, Clem?' asked Cleo, her eyebrows nearly touching her jagged blonde fringe.

'I'm not being mean, but have you gone a bit berserk, hon?' asked Chels.

Cleo grabbed me by the arm. 'Come on. We'll work this out. Obviously you're quite *upset.* It's okay. I have some trackies in my locker, and—'

I wrenched my arm away. 'Um, not to be mean or anything,' I said, 'but I'm actually happy with what I'm wearing. I don't want to wear your trackies. I wouldn't want to stretch them anyway.'

'Hon.' Chelsea-Grace put her hand on my other arm. 'You know we'd never—'

'It's okay.' I smiled. Something inside me had *unbuttoned.* I felt free. 'I know you're both just trying to help. But I also know I'd look terrible in your trackies, Cleo. They're pink. I'd look like a slightly overstuffed raw sausage. So it's lucky I look this hot in my gown, isn't it?'

'Well, I mean, you do look really pretty,' said Chels, 'but . . . but we don't understand why you're dressed like that. And, um, we don't understand why you left on Saturday? Brent is heartbroken. We just don't understand—'

'Me,' I interrupted. 'You don't understand me. You don't *know* me. At all. You never have.'

'Hey!' Cleo snapped. 'That's not true. We do know you. And we love you. And if we don't understand you, it's because you don't *let* us sometimes.'

'We're really sorry for how we reacted when Sam first hit on you,' said Chelsea-Grace softly. 'It's just that for ages now, we've felt . . . you're so *different*. From us. And we tried and tried to keep 3CD the same, together, but it was like you didn't want that. You didn't want to do stuff with us. You didn't want to be *like* us. We thought you were ashamed of us. And that was what upset us the most. You hurt us, Clem.' Tears clung to the ends of Chelsea-Grace's thick mascara.

I stared at her, open-mouthed. I didn't know what to say. Finally, I managed one word. 'How?'

'By keeping stuff from us,' said Chelsea-Grace. 'By thinking we wouldn't understand, about the smart books you were reading, or the, um, *interesting* music you like—'

'Or about Fergus. You never told us what was going on with Fergus,' Cleo added. Her chin was beginning to wobble, too. I hadn't seen Cleo cry since Beyoncé cancelled her Australian tour. 'He's like our big brother, Clem,' she said. 'And you never even tell us how he's going.'

'And we try to involve you in *our* lives, all the time – like with Brent and running and stuff. When the two of us decided we wanted to go on runs every couple of days, we asked you to come, too, because we thought it would be *nice*. To spend time together. Because we want you to be part of us again.' Tears were now rolling freely down Chelsea-Grace's cheeks, making glimmering tracks in her foundation.

'I'm . . . sorry,' I said. 'I didn't know you were feeling like that.'

'You never bothered to ask,' said Cleo, in a small voice. 'And now you come to school dressed like *that*—'

'It's for a boy,' I blurted. 'His name is Fred Paul.' Cleo and Chelsea-Grace looked perplexed. 'The boy under the gum tree,' I explained.

'The geek?' asked Chelsea-Grace. 'Sorry,' she said quickly when Cleo glared at her.

'You like him? Fred?' Cleo asked. I nodded.

'I like him a lot. We've actually been seeing each other.'

'What? This is what I mean!' cried Cleo. 'Why didn't you *tell* us? Why did you let us try to set you up with Brent?'

I shrugged. 'I guess I wanted to be close to you again, too.' When Cleo looked at me sceptically, I added, 'I really did. I thought you'd disapprove of Fred. That's why I didn't tell you about him. I certainly never meant to hurt you.'

'We would have understood,' Cleo said. 'We're not monsters.'

'I know,' I replied sheepishly.

Cleo nodded. 'Erm, but you still haven't quite explained the dress.'

And so I told them everything. About Fred, and BSS, and how Noel had seen me with Brent. About how I had to get Fred back. When I finished, I looked expectantly from Chels to Cleo, waiting for their reactions. They glanced at each other, and back at me.

'Can we walk you there?' asked Cleo.

'We'll hold your hand,' Chelsea-Grace added. 'Somebody has to carry that paint tin. It so doesn't match your outfit.'

'And . . . sorry for eavesdropping, but I am *so* coming too.'

I turned around. Gemma was standing behind me, dressed in a 'pulp mills stink' T-shirt and grinning from ear to ear.

'You look super-hot, Honeysuckle Nightingale. And I *knew* you'd never ditch Fred for some jock. Anybody can tell it's true love between the two of you! Let's roll!'

I felt as though I was going to burst with happiness and gratitude. I grabbed Chelsea-Grace's hand with my left one, and Cleo's with my right, and Gemma followed us, massaging my shoulders as if I was a heavyweight boxer about to step into the ring. And we walked together towards the cider gum.

I know you're probably thinking this is the climax. This is the part where I get my man.

But then how would you explain the red paint?

There's a wall by the art rooms, Ms Hiller.

You know the one. Fred mentioned it before. It's the one the art students use as a graffiti wall. They paint pictures and write motivational quotes on it, and the art teachers clean it back to a blank canvas once a month. I like that idea, Ms Hiller. The idea that every so often your life is wiped clean and you get a chance to create beautiful pictures on it all over again, write a new story of your existence. And I know Fred likes the idea, too. Which is why I took him there. Or, should I say, why *we* took him there.

It took the four of us, Ms Hiller, to get Fred away from the cider-gum tree and down to the art rooms.

We did it steampunk-style.

Cleo held up the note that I'd written in my best Victorian script.

Gemma blindfolded him.

And Chelsea-Grace whispered sweetly in his ear, 'I'm not trying to be mean, because it's just the truth: you're coming with us. Nice to finally meet you, by the way, Clementine's boyfriend. You're actually kind of hot, if weird. Don't take that the wrong—'

I had to interrupt. 'Chelsea-Grace? That wasn't in the script.'

'Sorry, Clem,' said Chels.

Before Fred had a chance to protest, I popped a very small, Victorian-era cake into his gaping mouth. And then we led him down to the art rooms.

Luke (Rosalinde's arty boyfriend) was waiting. 'I cleaned the wall, like you asked me to,' he whispered. 'Good luck, Clem.'

'We'll leave you to it now,' said Gemma, taking Chelsea-Grace by the hand when she looked reluctant to leave.

'I just have to say, though . . .' Cleo handed me back the paint tin. 'If you don't forgive this girl, Fred, you're an idiot. She's Helen of Troy. She's Boadicea. She's unsurpassable. She's phenomenal.'

'Right,' said Fred, wiping some crumbs from his mouth with the back of his hand.

Cleo winked at me, and the girls ran away together, giggling madly.

Once Fred and I were alone I took his blindfold off gently. He looked at me with a mixture of bemusement and fury.

'What in heaven's name are you doing?' he snapped. 'I didn't say anything in front of the other girls – because it would have been most ungentlemanly to do so – but I am very affronted by this whole situation. First you kiss the jock—'

'I never kissed the jock,' I interrupted. 'I promise,' I added. I hoped he could see in my eyes that I was telling the truth. Something in his face softened. And I let myself hope.

'Brent will back me up,' I said quickly. 'Nothing happened. I promise. I really, really promise.'

'Okay,' said Fred slowly. 'I believe you.'

'Really?' I asked, daring to let the hope become real.

Fred nodded. 'I am wondering, however, what the story is with the paint tin.'

'Sit,' I said. I set the tin down for a moment and opened my bag. I pulled out my old Décor lunch box, which was filled with Victorian cakes and pastries. Fergus had helped me find the recipes. 'Eat. And let me do the rest.'

And so, while Fred obligingly took a seat on the art hallway carpet, I opened the paint tin. And I wrote.

You
came from nowhere,
from the mists of time,
and made my life magical.
You
are winter sun,
are rushing wind,
are the smell of cinnamon
and cider gum.
You are newness.
You are life.
You are that thing
that woke me,
that imagined me,
a new Clementine.
You held my hand
as I wrote the first word
of a new story,
Writing Clementine.
You are this wall.
You are these words.
You are an adventure.
You are the first step.

I stopped painting then, Ms Hiller. I turned to Fred. He hadn't eaten a single cake. I might have been offended, but that smile . . . those dimples . . .

That kiss.

And then he took the paintbrush from my hand and he wrote on the wall, *Thank you*, and, *You're magical.*

And I confess, I kissed him again.

And that's when we spilled the paint. All over the both of us.

The Best Meal of My Life, Take Two! by Clementine Darcy

When I told Fergus that the dinner party was going to be bigger than I'd first planned, he didn't look frightened. He nodded seriously and said, 'I can do bigger. How many people?'

'Well, there's me and Fred and Mum and Dad and Sophie.' He nodded again. I took a deep breath. 'And then there's Ang and Lucy and Gemma, and Noel and Liam and Joshua. They're my steampunk friends. Fred told them about the dinner and they got so excited I *had* to ask them, too. And then Gemma said something about it in front of Chelsea-Grace and Cleo, so of course I couldn't let them feel excluded. And then Kerrard and Todd had to be invited – they're Chelsea-Grace and Cleo's boyfriends – and then Brent felt left out and so . . .'

I looked at Fergus warily. I was worried the expanded guest list might freak him out. But he tapped his chin thoughtfully. 'Doable,' he said. And then he surprised me again. 'Can I ask a friend? Just a guy I used to work with. He's started a new café and he reckons he might have some work for me. I thought he might like to see my mad skills in action.'

'Of course,' I said. 'I think that's a great idea.'

Here's what we ate at the steampunk dinner:

ENTRÉE

Julienne soup

MAIN

Filets de sole with creamed potatoes and greens
Lobster rissoles with mayonnaise of chicken
Saddle of mutton with minted peas and roasted root vegetables

DESSERT

Crepes with berry sauce
Caramel soufflé with preserved fruits
Bread-and-butter pudding with clotted cream

And everything was delicious, Ms Hiller. Everyone ate a huge amount, even Chelsea-Grace and Cleo! I think at first they tried everything because they were worried Fergus might cry if they didn't, but once they'd started, they couldn't stop. It was wonderful to see. It felt like they were being real for the first time in ages.

Sophie was a bit quiet, Ms Hiller. I couldn't help watching her; at times she seemed so far away. I liked to imagine she'd gone to the faerieland we used to escape to. I don't think that was the case, though. She looked as if she was about to cry. But you know, maybe those tears were good tears. Tears of relief. Of letting go.

So that's something.

In fact, the whole dinner party was full of little somethings. Like Fergus and Lucy exchanging small smiles at each other, and the way she blushed when he came close. Like Sophie and Brent talking up a friendly storm: first he managed to cheer away her impending tears, and by dessert he actually made her laugh! Like my serious lawyer mum trying to keep a straight face while wearing one of Lucy's too-big velvet dresses and a velvet bonnet on her sleek, serious lawyer bob. There are some people who were *meant* to live in the Victorian era, Ms Hiller. My mother is not one of them.

Like how, for the whole dinner party, Fred held my hand. And how, across the table, Mum was holding Dad's hand. They looked so happy to have their family together again for the first time in so long. And so proud of all of us.

As for Fergus, as he raced around the kitchen, stirring and whisking and frying and checking the oven, and then hovered around Lucy out in the dining room, asking her *constantly* if she was enjoying her food, he looked the happiest I have seen him in an awfully long time. And his friend with the café? He said Fergus's food was 'flawless'.

And I thought that maybe, just maybe, things might be all right again. Maybe not that night. Maybe not for weeks. But sometime soon.

After dinner, Mum and Dad told us that they were happy to do the washing up, and that we should go and 'be young', it being Friday night and all.

So we all hung out in the living room for a bit longer. And it was then that Kerrard, Todd and Brent persuaded Fred to go skating with them that Sunday.

'Uh, well, I'm not sure I'll be quite . . . attired for, uh, that, uh . . . ever,' Fred said, smoothing down his jodhpurs.

'Have you seen the rest of us?' laughed Kerrard, who had a top hat sitting awkwardly on top of his bleached dreadlocks. 'Come on. Don't be shy. Wear whatever the hell you like. It'll be fun!'

'Well . . . all right then,' said Fred. He looked happy and proud to be included, and my heart sang for him.

A little while later, the boys all headed off. The girls, it had been agreed upon, were staying over for a pyjama party. All of them. And Sophie had already shyly asked if she might join us.

'I'll see you tomorrow, right?' I said to Fred. 'At the ball?'

Fred nodded. 'I believe that Lucy, Ang and Gemma have been working on a special ensemble for you. I can't wait to see it.'

'Oh, you're going to look so awesome!' Ang giggled. She turned to Cleo and Chelsea-Grace. 'You should see her in her steampunk gear. The girl's a vixen!'

'We know,' said Cleo, smiling.

The other boys melted off into the cold night. I walked Fred out to the kerb, alone, and he kissed me gently on the cheek. 'I'm so glad to have met your family,' he said. 'And your friends.'

'Holy blueberry bagels. You're not going to ask them for my *hand* or anything now, are you?' I asked.

Fred laughed. 'No. You see, I have to ask for Madame le Chat's approval before I can do that. And that could take some time. She's a busy lady. It is very time-consuming, duelling with that musket-wielding husband of hers all the time. I might ask you to dance tomorrow night, though, if that's something you would like.'

'I think that *is* something I would like,' I said.

'Good night, Lady Nightingale,' he said, taking my hand and kissing it.

'Night, Freddie P,' I replied, and kissed him square on the mouth.

'I'm not sure that was entirely true to the behaviours of the period,' he scolded.

I raised my hands in the air. 'Sorry. I was just being a live fish.' I flapped my hands about like they were fins and puffed out my cheeks.

Fred shook his head. 'I will call the lunatic asylum in the morning. Although, actually, they will probably accuse you of hysteria and subject you to their revolutionary new treatment for insanity – they call it *lobotomy* – so perhaps I won't call them after all.' He poked out his tongue. 'I think I need you around here. After all, I really like you. I might even . . . love you.'

'I love you, too,' I said softly. 'In any era you choose to adventure in.'

Fred's grin grew huge, his dimples making dents in his cheeks.

'Well, I'd best be off, to prepare mentally for how a Victorian gentleman might go about *skateboarding*,' he said, making his fingers into quotation marks. 'I daresay that will be something of an adventure.'

'Take this with you,' I blurted, and I pressed another poem into his hand. So no, you can't see this one. I know the one I wrote him on the wall was public, but this poem is between me and the boy I love. Besides, I doubt you'd want to read it. It's a bit soppy.

'Look at it when you're alone,' I said. My cheeks were all aglow, like the fire from a Victorian steam train in the dark.

'I will,' Fred said. 'And . . . thank you. For trusting me.'

Then he kissed me on the cheek, and my whole body felt warm. Fred is the brightest fish in the stream, Ms Hiller. And the best.

He's at the desk in front of me now, still writing. I wonder if he's writing about me. I like the idea that he's making me with words; making me the way he sees me. Writing Clementine.

I wonder if he'll let me read it someday.

I don't know what else to write now. There are five minutes left of class.

Blue fish, red fish, green fish . . .

Blue fish, red fish, green fish . . .

I'll have more to write tomorrow, I'm sure, Ms Hiller. I can't wait to find out what happens next, and I bet you can't either.

Let's see where my fins will take me.

Are you curious, Ms Hiller?

Acknowledgements

First and foremost, I have to thank my husband, Leigh. If it wasn't for him, not only would this book not exist, but none of them would. If it wasn't for him, in fact, I would not be a writer at all.

My family, too (the Lovells and the Gordons), must be thanked for the simple fact that they are every bit as awesome as the family in this book. My dad wrote me the first stories I loved, stories set in Tasmania. I write because of him and for him. My mum surrounded me with books growing up and made them my family. My new Gordon family have read my stories and shared them around the world, and I will be forever grateful for their love and acceptance.

Nanette Halliday was my agent when I began writing this novel. She was my agent from the beginning, but she was more than 'just' an agent. She was my mentor, my voice of reason, my confidante, my cheer squad. I miss having her as my agent. I hope I'll always have her as my friend. I am very glad to have Brian Cook in my corner as my new agent from this book forwards!

Nansi and Sam, my little critterbugs, this is for you, too. You are talented. You are kind. You are fabulous.

Mr Hiller, in your navy-blue jumper, with that amazing world inside your head, thank you for being the inspiration for this story. I've been lucky enough to have many phenomenal teachers in my life. Two of them stand out above the rest.

My high school English teacher, Mr Wilson, was one of them. He taught me to write. You taught me to imagine.

Jodie and Elise, what would I have done without you two? Editors are the best of people, and you are the best of editors. I am so proud to be part of your Onion family and so grateful to have your wisdom, kindness and support in this crazy, wonderful business called writing.

Arts Tasmania, wow, what would I have done without you? Tassie is such a lucky, lucky place to have such a dedicated organisation working to assist and promote its arts scene, and I am so very grateful for all the help you've given me in my career so far. I wouldn't have a career without you!

Lastly, my Tiger. Ever since you came into this world, everything I have done has been for you. This is no exception. You are the cat's pyjamas, sweetheart. I hope you read this one day and are proud of your mummy.

Oh, and you lovely, lovely people who read these stories? You, each of you, are beautiful and inspiring and magic. I am so indebted to you all. Thank you all. You make my world.

About the Author

Kate Gordon lives in Hobart, in a mint-green cottage, with her husband, her very strange cat, Mephy Danger Gordon, and a wonderful, mad little girl, who goes by the name of Tiger. Kate dreams that one day she and her little family will live in another cottage, by the beach, with goats and chickens. In the meantime, she fills her house with books, perfects her gluten-free baking technique, has marvellous adventures with Tiger, and she writes. She is the author of *Three Things About Daisy Blue* (Girlfriend Fiction), *Thyla* and *Vulpi*.

Kate was the recipient of 2011 and 2012 Arts Tasmania Assistance to Individuals grants, which means she can now spend more time doing what she loves.